NEW YORK TIMES BESTSELLING AUTHOR
KAYLEE RYAN

BLISS
Copyright © 2020 Kaylee Ryan

All Rights Reserved.
This book may not be reproduced in any manner whatsoever without the written permission of Kaylee Ryan, except for the use of brief quotations in articles and or reviews.

This book is a work of fiction. Names, characters, events, locations, businesses and plot are products of the author's imagination and meant to be used in a fictitious manner. Any resemblance to actual persons, living or dead, or actual events throughout the story are purely coincidental. The author acknowledges trademark owners and trademarked status of various products referenced in this work of fiction, which have been used without permission. The publication and use of these trademarks are not authorized, sponsored or associated by or with the trademark owners.

The following story contains sexual situations and strong language. It is intended for adult readers.

Cover Design: Sommer Stein, Perfect Pear Creative Covers
Cover Photography: Braadyn Penrod
Editing: Hot Tree Editing
Proofreading: Deaton Author Services
Formatting: Integrity Formatting

PART TWO

Bliss

Chapter 1

COOPER

I can't breathe. It physically hurts to pull oxygen into my lungs. There's a tightness in my chest that I'm afraid will never go away. My hands tightly grip the chair in front of me as I watch Reese walk down the aisle. She's beautiful, but there was never a doubt that she'd be a vision in a wedding dress. For a minute, I thought she might not go through with it. When our eyes met, and I mouthed to her that I loved her, I thought maybe, just maybe for a fleeting second that she was going to call it all off.

Instead, I watched as she, with her father at her side, put one foot in front of the other, passing me by to go to him. To Hunter. My body is frozen as I watch her. With each step she takes, it's as if a dagger is piercing my heart.

I don't want to watch this, but she asked me to be here. I will never again deny her anything. The one time I did has become my biggest regret in life. I had her, in my bed, in my arms, and I pushed her away. That's a mistake that I have to learn to live with, and one I will damn sure never be making again. I should have told her sooner. Just something else to add to my growing list of regrets.

I can't look away, no matter how badly I want to. I need to see her do this. I need to listen to her tell him that she vows to love him forever, so that maybe, just maybe, my heart will get the message that she's not ours.

"Who gives this woman to marry this man?" the preacher asks once Reese and Garrett reach the altar.

"Don't do it," I whisper under my breath. Surely Garrett knows she's meant to be mine. I watch as Garrett brings her hand to his lips and kisses it lightly. He then takes her hand and places it in Hunter's.

Did you hear that? That loud crack is my heart as it breaks? Millions of shattered pieces that will never be the same, not without Reese.

"Her mother and I do," Garrett says proudly. He steps away and takes his seat on the front row next to Eve.

My mother is sitting next to Eve, and my father next to her. There's an empty seat next to my father. It's the seat I was supposed to sit in. I just… couldn't. I'm having a hard enough time sitting in the back row. I would be too tempted to drop to my knees in front of her and beg her not to go through with it. Who am I kidding? The temptation is still there.

I texted my parents to let them know I was here but sitting in the back. Mom tried to convince me to come sit with them, but I just can't. I know they know that this day is hard for me, but they have no idea the depths of the agony I'm in. They don't know that she's my heart, and my best friend. They don't know that her father isn't the only one giving her away. I'm losing her, and the pain of that steals my breath from my lungs.

"Dearly beloved," the preacher begins.

Closing my eyes, I say a silent prayer that when I open them, this will have been a nightmare. That I won't be sitting in the back row of this banquet hall, and the love of my life won't be about to pledge her love for someone else.

Slowly, I open my eyes.

I'm still here.

She's still there.

With a man who's not me.

"If anyone can show just cause why this couple cannot lawfully be joined together in matrimony, let them speak now or forever hold their peace." The question echoes throughout the quiet room.

My nails dig into the back of the chair in front of me. I need to say something. I can't let her do this. I need to stand up and shout out that she's making a mistake. No one can love her like I can. My grip is so tight on the chair, my knuckles are white, and I'm losing feeling in my hands. I bite down on my bottom lip to keep from yelling out, or hell, maybe it's to keep my tears at bay. I can feel them brewing as the heat builds behind my eyes.

Steadying my weight on my hands, I push up from my chair at the same time Reese looks out into the crowd. She searches until her eyes lock on mine, causing my heart to stall in my chest. I open my mouth to speak but quickly close it. Instead, I watch as she removes her hands from Hunter's and takes a small step back. Her hand shoots out behind her, and Tessa hands her something.

I need to do it now, before she goes any further. My mouth is dry, almost as if it's been stuffed with cotton. I swallow a few times and lick my lips. Here goes nothing. I open my mouth to speak, but her words stop me.

"Hunter. I'm sorry. I- I can't do this," she says as her voice cracks.

There's a collective gasp throughout the room. Low murmurs of surprise ring out while I still stand frozen in the back row, on the left side. The bride's side. I don't take my eyes off her as I will her to look at me. She's up there doing this all on her own, and I want to be with her. I want to stand beside her, my head held tall as she makes this announcement.

I want to do all of that, but my feet won't move. It's as if they're glued to the floor, and all I can do is stand and watch this play out. Hunter reaches for her, but she takes another step back and shakes her head. I can see the tremble in her hands as she removes her engagement ring from her left hand and places it in his.

Her mouth is moving, but I can't hear what she's saying. She drops her hands to her sides and looks over her shoulder at Tessa. I see it all in slow motion as she turns on her heel and rushes to the side of the room, disappearing behind the door. I watch her go, with Tessa hurrying along behind her.

The door slams closed behind Tessa, and suddenly the crowd grows louder. All I can do is stare at the door. I wanted this to happen, but she's hurting, and I hate that. I need to go to her. I need to hold her in my arms and tell her that everything is going to be okay. I need to show her how much I love her and support her through this.

Shaking out of my fog, I slowly release my grip on the chair in front of me and flex my hands, helping to circulate the blood flow. I move to take a step, but a firm hand presses on my shoulder. Turning to look, I see Nixon standing there.

"Come with me," he says, keeping his voice low.

"I can't. I have to go to her." I shake my head.

"She's with Tess, and your best bet of finding out where that is, is through me. Let's go." With his hand on my arm, he pulls me behind him. We rush through the double doors and down the hall that leads outside.

"Where are we going? I'm not leaving. I have to go to her. Damn it, Nix, Let go!" I yell into the parking lot.

"They left, Cooper. She's not here. Now shut the hell up and get in the car."

"What do you mean they left? How could she have just left that soon? Where did they go?" I fire off a multitude of questions.

"Get in the fucking car, Cooper," he says through gritted teeth as the door we just escaped through opens.

"Cooper!" Garrett calls out.

I give Nixon a pleading look, and he mutters, "Fuck," under his breath. I turn to look at Garrett.

"Where is she?" he calls out as he approaches.

"We're going to her now." That's really all I've got.

He nods. His eyes darting between Nixon and me. I know I should say something like I've got this, and I'll take care of her, but the truth is, I'm not sure where they are, and I have no idea what I'm up against. I wanted her to call it off, but this… her running out, that's not Reese. My chest is heavy from guilt, but there is also a sense of relief that washes over me. Both emotions pulling in equal measures.

I want her to be mine.

"Take care of her, Cooper." Garrett gives me a hard look that's also a little pleading.

I look him square in the eyes. "Always," I say with conviction and promise. There will never be a moment in my life that I won't put her first. Never.

"Cooper. We need to go," Nixon says.

I give Garrett a firm nod and climb in the car. "Where are they?" I ask Nixon as he speeds out of the parking lot.

"I'm not sure."

"What the fuck do you mean you're not sure? Stop the car. I can't leave her here."

"She's not there, Cooper." He tosses me his phone and rattles off the password. "Pull up the last message from Tess."

Doing as he says, I pull up the text messages on his phone.

> **Tess:** We're leaving. She's really upset and not saying much. I don't know where we're headed, but I do know we won't be going back to the banquet hall.
>
> **Nixon:** I'll get Cooper. You tell me when and where.

"So, what?" I say, frustrated and tossing his phone in the cupholder. "We're just going to drive around until we know where they are?"

"You have a better plan? Would you rather be back there dealing with the aftermath? The way that you were looking at her...." He shakes his head.

"What?" I ask, the irritation evident in my voice. "Say it." I need to hear it.

"The fucking agony was written all over your face, Reeves. Not one person there could question whether or not her marrying Hunter was tearing you up inside."

"I told her I would never hide how I felt about her again. That included showing that my fucking heart was obliterated that she was marrying someone who wasn't me."

"What are you saying, Reeves? That you want to marry her."

"Yes." I don't even hesitate with my response.

He pulls up to a Stop sign and turns to look at me. "You're serious." It's not a question as much as a statement of observation.

"Yes."

He nods. "All right. I'll do what I can to help you. Tess too. She's been insistent for years that the two of you should be together."

"Is that where you got it?" I ask him.

"Nah, I could see it too. In fact, I think everyone around the two of you could see it. I think even Hunter knew. Deep down, he had to know," he says.

"I feel bad for the guy, getting left at the altar sucks, but I'm fucking thrilled she did it. That makes me a dick, right? That I'm happy she didn't go through with it?"

"Nah, makes you human. Although you should have told her a hell of a lot sooner than the day before her wedding."

"I was struggling." I know he's right. I should have told her sooner. The day I got that fucking wedding invitation, I should have told her. Instead, I stayed holed up in my condo and got wasted. Not my finest moment, but my heart was breaking. I'd lost her. I hate that it took me going off to Indy without her for me to see the perfect woman for me had been right in front of me for years. It took me being without her to realize she can still be my best friend and the love of my life.

"Stubborn," he mutters under his breath.

Maybe he's right. I don't really know. What I do know is that I'm going to do everything in my power to show her what she means to me. No more pushing her away or wishing things were different. I'm going to show her every fucking day.

Nixon's phone rings, and he snatches it up before I can get it. "Hello." He listens. "Yeah, I've got Cooper with me." Another pause. "Okay. We're on our way." He hangs up and places the phone back in the cupholder and continues to drive.

"Where are they?"

"The hotel that Tess and I are staying at."

"Whose car are they in?"

He looks over at me and grins. "A rental."

"Isn't this a rental?" I ask of the sedan we're in.

"Yep," he says, popping the *p*.

"Why did you and Tessa have two rentals?"

"We didn't until this morning."

"Care to enlighten me?"

He chuckles. "The one we rented this morning is the getaway car."

"What do you mean?" I ask, confused.

"Tess had a feeling that Reese was struggling and didn't really want to go through with the wedding. She insisted we have a car parked out back, and she had the keys. That's what Reese took from her when they were standing up there. Tessa told her about the keys and that she had them in her hands. All Reese had to do was ask."

"Thank you." Those two words don't seem like enough, but right now, that's all I've got. I wish I would have thought of it, but it's better it was Tessa.

The rest of the ride to the hotel is silent. I'm lost in thought. I don't know what I'm going to say to her when I see her. Hell, I don't even know if she's willing to see me. That's not going to stop me from trying.

Nixon pulls up to the valet, and we climb out of the car. Hands in my pockets, I follow him like a lost puppy through the lobby and to the elevators. I don't say a word on the ride up, or when the doors open and he steps off. We finally stop outside a room, and he knocks softly. My breathing halts as I wait for them to answer. What feels like hours later, when it's merely seconds, Tessa opens the door and gives us a sad smile.

"H-How is she?" I ask, my voice gravelly.

"As good as can be expected after running out of her own wedding."

I wince. "Can I see her?"

"Depends. Tell me you're in this for the long haul, Cooper."

"Eternity."

She nods and hands me a card. "I got you a room too. I wasn't sure where you were staying, and well, I'm not sure how this is going to go over. I was hoping that would be your answer, and you would want to be close to her. Your room is there." She points across the hall. "We're a few floors up. Call us if you need anything."

"Thanks, Tessa." Pulling my hands from my pockets, I take the offered card with a mental note to repay them and wrap my arms around her in a hug.

"Hands off my wife, Reeves," Nixon says. His voice is calm and holds no heat.

"She's not your wife yet," I fire back.

"Close enough. Go get yours," he says, drawing Tessa into his arms. I watch as he kisses the top of her head, and together, arms wrapped around one another, they head down the hall.

Slowly, I push open the door and walk in, making sure to lock it behind me. With each step I take into the room, my heart seems to pound a little faster. By the time I can see her, I feel as though it might pound right out of my chest.

"Reese," I say, my voice gruff like sandpaper.

She looks up at me with tears staining her cheeks, and red, watery eyes. I don't give her a chance to speak or to even act before I'm rushing to her, dropping to my knees and cradling her face in the palm of my hands.

"I'm so sorry, baby," I whisper as my thumbs swipe across her cheeks, drying her tears. I hate to see her like this. I hate it's because of me. I should have told her sooner. This is my fault, and I'll do anything to make it up to her.

"I don't know what's happening, Cooper."

"We'll figure it out together," I tell her.

"Will we?" She pushes my hands away and stands as she begins to pace the room. "I can't believe you dropped all this on me the day before my wedding. Do you know how incredibly selfish that is? That you don't want me, but you don't want him to have me, so you make up this bullshit story about being in love with me? Who does that?"

"It's not bullshit, Reese." I stand, and again have to shove my hands in my pockets to keep from reaching for her.

"It is!" she screams. "Why now, Cooper? Huh? Why all of a sudden do you want me? You say you're *in* love with me? What changed?"

"I changed." I take one step closer to her and stop. "I changed because I learned what life was like without you in it. It fucking sucks, Reese. I hate it. I think about you every fucking second of every day, and it's not because you're my best friend. It's because you're my fucking soul." My hands fly out of my pockets as I smack my chest. 'Right fucking here." I tap my heart. "That's where you live, and frankly, I can't live without you. I don't want to. I'm miserable."

"You're miserable?" She scoffs. "I threw myself at you, and you turned me away. You didn't want me. I was trying to move on. I was supposed to be married to a good man who would always want me, and now this?" She waves her hands around the room. "I'm here in my fucking wedding dress fighting with you."

"I don't want to fight with anyone else." My voice is low, but her eyes soften just a little, as does her posture at my words. I take another step toward her. "I'm in love with you, Reese. Not because you've been my best friend since I was eight years old. Not because I don't want anyone else to have you. Although that's true. You're mine. I love you because of the way my heart races at just hearing your name." I take another step toward her. "I love your smile and your laugh. I love the way that no matter where you are in a room, I can feel you." I take one final step that leaves me toe to toe with her. Placing my index finger under her chin, I tilt her head up so we're eye to eye. "I love you for this." Reaching out, I grab her hand and place it over my racing heart. "I love that you are in here. You live inside of me, Reese. I never want that to change. Ever. I want to spend the rest of my life showing you how much I love you."

"Coop," she cries, as big fat tears run unchecked down her face.

"Don't cry, baby. I'm right here." I wrap my arms around her, pulling her to my chest. Sobs rack her body as she clings to me. I hate that she's hurting and I'm the cause of that pain, but at the same time, I'm so fucking grateful she's here in my arms, and I have the chance to love her like she deserves to be loved. "I love you, Reese," I whisper, pressing my lips to the top of her head.

Her sobs turn to sniffles and eventually quiet, and she lifts her head from my chest to look at me. Green eyes filled with sadness, love, confusion, and worry stare back at me. I want to ease her fears, and the only way I can do that is to show her. Sliding one hand behind her neck, I bend, pressing my lips to hers. Just a feather-soft touch to gauge the moment.

"Coop," she breathes, and suddenly there's something else in those beautiful eyes of hers.

Desire.

My hands settle on her waist as I bring her body flush with mine. She moans, and I have to taste her. This time I take what I want. I push my tongue past her lips and explore her mouth. My hands roam up and down her back, tracing her spine. She whimpers, and all bets are off. I need her naked.

Now.

Pulling back, I move us to the bed. She stands still as she watches me rip off my suit jacket and toss it on the floor. I remove my shirt from my dress pants and fumble with the button, and then the zipper as I tug them over my hips, letting them pool around my ankles. I kick off my shoes, and then my pants, as I rip open my shirt. Buttons ping off the walls as they fly across the room, but I couldn't care less. I get to the neck and realize I'm still wearing my tie. With deft fingers, I work the knots and slide it over my head, dragging my shirt off and tossing it to the floor as well.

I'm standing before her in nothing but my boxer briefs, which do nothing to hide the fact that my cock is hard and aching for her. "I love you." My voice is strong and doesn't waver. I watch her closely, and her breathing accelerates at my confession. "I need you out of this fucking dress," I growl. It kills me to see her in the dress she bought to wear for him. "Turn around, baby."

She does as I ask. Kissing the back of her neck, I start with the zipper. As wedding dresses go, this one is simple. White, silk, and landing just above her ankles. There is no flair, or princess qualities—something I always thought of when I thought of Reese in a wedding gown. Over the past couple of months, since I got the invitation, I've imagined it quite often, and every time I was the man waiting for her at the altar.

Me.

I need her out of this one. The dress she bought to wear for him. With trembling hands, I give the zipper a tug, and nothing happens. I try again and still nothing. With a heavy sigh, I rest my forehead against her shoulder.

"Coop," she says, reaching her arms behind her and grabbing my cock. "I need you." There's a tremor in her voice, a need I must cater to.

Only me.

Her words send fire coursing through my veins. She needs me, and that's more than I could ever ask for. I want to be that man for her. The one she can lean on, and the one who fuels her desires. The one who gives her everything she needs, in the bedroom and in life.

Fuck it.

Lifting my head, I grip either side of the dress by the zipper and tug. The silk fabric tears. Reese gasps, the sound echoing throughout the room. With the fabric still gripped tightly in my fists, I pull until the dress falls from her body. Underneath, I find my Reese wearing a white lace thong and matching bra. It's as if she's a gift, not just to me but to my heart, and my cock, one we can't wait to unwrap.

"I don't know where to start," I murmur, raking my eyes over her body. She makes the decision for me when she slides her fingers into the waistband of her thong. She shimmies her hips, and the tiny piece of fabric slides to the floor. When she reaches behind her back to unclasp her bra, I place my hands over hers, stopping her. "Let me." My voice is low and husky. I've thought about this moment a thousand times. Finally, after years of hiding and denying my attraction to her, we've come to this.

"Cooper," she whispers.

I lean in and kiss the back of her neck, my lips trailing over to her bare shoulder. I want my lips on every inch of her skin. I want to trace every curve. I want to memorize her. Then, I want to do it all again. Over and over again, every fucking day for the rest of my life.

Unsnapping her bra, I slide the straps over her shoulders. I watch as she removes each arm and tosses the white lace to the floor. I don't bother to look where it lands. No, my eyes are glued to her smooth, silky skin. When I reach out with my index finger between her breasts, she shivers. "You cold, baby?" I ask, my voice thick.

She turns to face me. Her eyes, although still red from her tears, are filled with longing.

"I lo—" I start to tell her again, but she rises on the balls of her feet and presses her lips to mine. I can feel the tremble in her hands as she presses them to my bare chest.

The time for talking is done. Time to show her how much I love her.

Chapter 2

REESE

I'm an entangled mess of emotions. I'm supposed to be celebrating my nuptials with Hunter, the man I was engaged to just hours earlier, yet here I am, in a hotel room with my best friend. My best friend who decided the day before my wedding to tell me he's in love with me. I don't know if I believe him. I know Cooper, and he's always been protective of me. He's never thought that anyone was good enough for me, and I have a strong suspicion that's what this is about.

Regardless, his confession of love made me think. In fact, thinking is all I was able to do all last night, and throughout the day. I came to the conclusion that I didn't want to marry Hunter. He's a great guy, but he was safe. When Cooper pushed me away, I was broken, and Hunter was sweet, and never pressured me. Hell, he had his own beliefs. We respected one another, but I don't love him. Not like I should.

I just walked out on my wedding, and I'm more torn up about the fact that Cooper is here telling me he loves me. I'm upset because I want more than anything for his words to be true, but I just can't trust them. He's broken my heart in the past. I kept that from him. The pain, the agony he caused. I never let the pain show. That's my mistake, my issue, and I need to be honest with him, and I will be.

However, for once, I'm being selfish. I want him. I want to know what it feels like to have his body pressing into mine. I want to know what it feels like to be a part of him. For us to be one together. I've fantasized about him for years, and I'm giving in to temptation. He's here, and he's willing. I'm here, and this is all I've ever wanted. I know there is so much we need to discuss. There is still so much I need to figure out. I need time to process all of this.

After tonight.

Tonight, for the first time in my life, I'm taking what I want. What my heart really wants. And that's Cooper. I know it's wrong, but I can't seem to find it in me to care. My life has been flipped upside down in the last twenty-four hours. I've always wanted him, and even though he's here under the guise that our lives are now entwined, I know better. However, I'm still taking this moment. I'll need it to carry me through the heartbreak and the tears once he realizes he was wrong. That he was just jealous of my time with Hunter, the time he was no longer getting.

This time, I'm not going to hide the hurt. I'm not going to sugarcoat it to spare his feelings. I need to put me first, and that includes being honest with how he broke me. I don't know what we will be after tonight. I don't know if I'm tossing away years of friendship for one night of being consumed by him, but it's a risk I'm willing to take. After this moment, after his confession of love, things have already changed. I know they'll never be the same.

I'm taking what I can get.

Cooper pulls out of the kiss, and we're both panting as we try and catch our breath. He smiles down at me, tucking my hair behind my ear. He's being sweet and affectionate, which is how I always imagined this moment would go. The only problem is, if I let this night continue down that path, my heart will never recover. The odds are against me as it is. My heart is so entwined with him that I know the scars of the past will always remain.

"You're beautiful," he says softly. His brown eyes are hooded as he takes in my naked body.

I'd love to stand here and let him tell me all the sweet things he thinks he needs to say, but again, I know my heart and know I can't take it. Placing my hands flat on his chest, I allow them to roam over the peaks and valleys he calls abs. Not able to handle the intensity of his stare, I allow my eyes to follow the path of my hands until I reach the waistband of his boxer briefs. His hard cock is peeking out the top. Gently, I trace the tip with my thumb, causing him to groan. With one hand held tightly to my hip, the other slides behind my neck as he leans down and presses his forehead to mine.

"Reese," he croaks. "Baby, as much as I love you touching me, we can't go there. Not right now. This can't be over before it starts."

Ignoring his words, I drop to my knees, pulling his boxer briefs down with me.

"Fuck," he mutters.

Wrapping my hand around him, I stroke him a couple of times, causing his legs to shake. I know he's about to stop me, so I lean in and take him into my mouth.

"Motherfucker," he pants. His hands bury in my hair, and I take as much of him as I can. He's long and thick, which makes it more difficult. When I pull back to get a better angle, he steps back. "No more," he rasps. "Not this time."

Glancing up at him, I see his chest rapidly rising and falling, the intensity of his breathing matching my own. I watch in fascination as he grips his hard length and tugs, much harder and faster than I was just moments before. "Get on the bed, Reese." It's not a request. It's a command.

A thrill races through me. Finally. After years of imagining being with him like this, it's going to happen. I push the possible consequences of my actions to the back of my mind. I want this. I want him, and now is the time. It's time to live in the moment and make up for the regrets of my past. I should have been more assertive that night. I should have told him what I wanted, but I shied away with his rejection.

I don't want to be that girl. I don't want to settle. Not anymore. Not this time.

"I wanted to take my time with you," he says, staring down at me. My eyes dart to where he strokes himself hard and fast. "Fuck, I can't do it. Not with you looking at me like that. Next time." There is promise in his voice. "On the bed, Reese."

I do as he says and climb onto the bed. Resting my head back against the pillow with my arms at my sides, I fight the urge to reach for the cover to pull it over me, but when his heated gaze captures mine, the thought disappears. I like the way he's looking at me. His stare is intense and causes me to shiver with anticipation.

Cooper releases his hard cock and bends to retrieve his pants. I watch with rapt attention as he shuffles for his wallet. When he finds it, he drops his pants to the floor as he searches and searches, coming up empty. "Fuck." He runs his hands through his hair, dropping his wallet to the floor, and looks up at me. I see the apology all over his face. "I don't have a condom."

"Seriously?" I ask. I would have thought that would be a staple for a man like him, you know, being a sexy professional athlete. I know women throw themselves at him. I've watched it happen for years. I can only imagine that's increased tenfold with his position on the Indianapolis Defenders.

"You think I planned this?" he asks, the hurt evident in his voice. "Reese, I was coming here to watch the love of my life marry another man. Getting laid was the last thing on my mind."

His words cause my heart to skip a beat. "Are you clean?"

"Of course I am." He scoffs as if me asking offended him.

"How long has it been?" I don't really think I want to know the answer to this question, but for us to move forward, I need to know.

"A long fucking time," he murmurs.

"How long is a long fucking time?" I ask. I'm sure our ideas of long are different.

He blows out a breath, closes his eyes, and looks to the ceiling. His hands move to his hips, and his hard cock stands tall and proud against the ridges of his abs. "Eyes up here," he says when he catches me ogling him.

"How long, Cooper?" I ask, not an ounce of shame for staring. This is my night, and it's my last with him, so I'm getting the full experience.

"High school," he mutters.

What did he just say? No way I heard him right. I open my mouth to ask him to repeat it, but his words stop me. "Senior prom, Reese. I never knew if someone was interested in me or my career, and then when I left, all I could think about was you."

"Me?" I croak. I'm floored by his words. I would never have believed it had I not heard it straight from his mouth. I know Cooper, and I know he's telling me the truth. How is it possible that it's been that long for him?

"Yes, you." His brown eyes soften. "You are the love of my life, Reese. I'm sorry it took me this long to tell you. That it took me this long to admit it to myself. I'll never make that mistake again. I promise you that." He pauses. "Are you on the pill?" he asks, swallowing hard.

"Yes, but just the last month or so."

"Oh."

"I'm clean too."

He nods. He thinks he understands, but he has no idea. "Okay." He nods, accepting my reply as my truth.

"Cooper." He's staring at the floor until his eyes pop to mine. "I didn't sleep with Hunter."

"What?" he asks, his eyebrows furrowed. "I don't understand. How is that even possible?"

"It's been since high school for me as well. Prom, senior year." It sounds crazy even to me that neither of us have expanded our sexual experience since we were seniors in high school. He says it was me, and I know my lack of experience is because all I wanted was him.

"It should have been me," he says with both sadness and conviction in his voice. "I wish with everything in me that I would have seen what I had right in front of me. It should have only ever been me." His voice drips with sincerity.

There is so much that just passed between us, so much information provided in just a matter of minutes, that I can't process it right now. I don't even want to try. I want him. He wants me. That's what matters in this moment. "I'm clean, and we're protected."

"You sure about this, baby?" His question is softly spoken, but the underlying need in his voice is evident.

"Have you changed your mind?"

"No." He's quick to answer. "Never."

"Then show me."

His eyes heat, and I know my words are what he needed to hear. In the blink of an eye, he's lying on the bed next to me. His large calloused hand cups one breast, then the other. "The thought of being inside you,

Bliss | 17

it's intimidating as fuck, but what's more is the thought of being inside of you bare. I know I'm not going to last."

"You don't know that," I whisper as his hand roams over my belly and slides between my thighs.

"I do know that. I was worried before, making love to you, the woman I love, for the first time, but this, knowing I get to feel all of you, all of this," he says, sliding a finger inside me, "It's more than I can handle. I know that."

"So you don't want me?" I ask, and no matter how hard I try to hide the hurt, it's there, sounding loud and clear in my voice.

"I'll always want you, Reese. Don't ever question that. I know I pushed you away, but that's not going to happen ever again." He lazily pumps his finger inside me. "I'll always want you, and I'll always love you. There's nothing in this world that will ever change that."

"So where does that leave us?" I ask, arching my back as he slides another digit inside me.

"That leaves me horny as fuck and dripping with need." He presses his hips into my thigh, and I can feel the precum on the tip of his cock on my leg. "That means I have to get you off because there are no promises the first time I feel you."

Reaching down, I wrap my fist around him and stroke. "I'll take my chances."

"You deserve better, baby. Let's just go ahead and make it known that you come first. Always."

I have to bite down on my lip to keep the sob that threatens to escape locked inside. He keeps talking about this like we're forever, and I wish that were true. I don't know how long I'll have him like this. Open and willing to be with me. We've made it further than before, and I want it all. I want all of him at least once before he gets scared again and runs.

"I need you," I pant as his fingers pump in and out of me. My body tenses and the fire ignites from deep inside.

"Fuck, Reese. I need you too. More than you'll ever know." Bending his head, he captures a nipple in his mouth and sucks hard. A moan from somewhere deep inside falls from my lips, and it only fuels him on. His hand pumps faster, and his teeth nip at my breasts before he soothes the ache with his tongue.

I can feel a deep twinge as the fire steadily builds. My grip on his cock tightens while the other hand grips the sheets on the bed.

"Easy, beautiful," he murmurs, his lips next to my ear.

Realizing I could be hurting him, I let go and reach for his arm instead. "Cooper," I moan as my body climbs closer and closer to release.

"Give it to me, Reese. Come all over my hand," he whispers in my ear.

As if his words press a magic button, my orgasm spirals out of control. I have a death grip on his arm, and the sheets, as my back arches off the bed, as the deep timbre of his voice tells me how much he loves me. It all flows through me at the same time as my release.

Bliss

I have no other words to describe the feeling other than pure, uninhibited bliss. My body seems to sink into the mattress, but I know there's still more to come. This time, I get all of him, and I'm ready. I've *been* ready. Slowly, I open my eyes to find his face close to mine, his eyes burning with desire. His gaze is intense.

"Hi," he whispers.

"Hi." I reach out and run my fingers through his hair. I wish I knew what was going through his head. Regardless, I'm not letting him turn me away. Not this time. Knowing I need to be brave, braver than I feel, I open my legs, making room for him. "I'm ready, Coop."

"Yeah," he agrees, as he finally pulls his fingers from inside me and brings them to his lips. I watch as he sucks each one into his mouth, his heated brown eyes never leaving mine. Once he's taken his time, he moves to settle between my legs. His fist, the same one that was just between my thighs, palms his cock as he gives himself a few leisurely strokes.

"Let me," I say, reaching between us.

"No." His voice is firm, but there is a small smile playing on his lips. "This is going to be embarrassing enough, baby. Your hands on me will not help."

I settle for resting my hands on his shoulders and pulling him down to me. He settles between my thighs, resting his weight on his elbows on either side of my head. Drawing him into a kiss, I wrap my legs around his waist and hold on tight.

"Jesus," he mutters, breaking the kiss.

"Please, Coop."

He nods and reaches between us and slowly guides his hard length inside me. My legs lock around his back, causing him to sink in deep, and we both moan our appreciation for the feeling of finally being connected. At least that's where mine is coming from.

Leisurely, he pulls out and then pushes back in. "You're so tight," he says through gritted teeth, "and so wet," he adds with another leisurely pump of his hips. Lifting my hips, I squeeze, and his eyes roll back in his head. "You can't do that. I'm so close," he mumbles, dropping his head to press his lips to mine.

"I want you to come." It's true. I want to know that he's losing himself inside me.

"You first." He smirks and slides his hand between us.

"I-I did," I pant as his thumb circles my clit.

"I know, but I need to feel you come around me." As soon as he says the words, his hips thrust as he picks up his pace. There is nothing relaxed about the way he's pushing inside of me. His thumb continues to slowly circle my clit, and his hips never lose rhythm.

All I can do… all I want to do is hold on for the ride. Sliding my hands under his arms, I dig my nails into his back, and he hisses.

"Fuck yes." He thrusts harder, pressing his thumb a little firmer, and that's when I feel it. The slow burn, the steady quake that begins to build as he thrusts.

"Coop-er," I breathe, feeling it. I'm so close. This one is stronger than the one before it. "Do-Don't stop." *Please, God, don't let him stop.*

"Come for me, Reese. I need you to come now," he grits out, and I ignite into flames. Heat courses through my veins as my body spasms around his.

"F-uckkkk!" He moans as he thrusts deep and stills, letting himself go inside me. He buries his face in my neck. I can feel his hot breath as it comes in spurts against my skin. When he's caught his breath, he slides out of me, and lies next to me on the bed, pulling me into his arms. "I love you, Reese."

His words are a whispered confession, but they still cause my heart to squeeze painfully. I want to say them back. I do love him. I will always love him, but I can't do that. I can't open myself up to him like that again, only for him to realize now I'm not getting married that he's made a mistake.

So I say nothing.

Instead, I close my eyes and listen to his breathing. Eventually, it evens out, and I know he's asleep, then and only then, do I allow myself to close my eyes.

COOPER

My eyes pop open as I lie still, listening for what woke me up. I don't hear anything, but now I'm awake, the memories of last night come at me full force. *Reese.* Last night was a surprise, and it was the best night of my life. I'll never forget it as long as I live. Needing to hold her, I roll over to cuddle up next to Reese. Only when I reach for her, she's gone.

I sit up in bed, the covers pooling around my waist as I survey the dimly lit room from the early morning sun. Her dress I tore off her body is gone, her shoes nowhere to be found. All that's left is a neatly folded pile of my clothes in the chair, my shoes and socks stacked neatly underneath.

Throwing the covers off, I stalk to the bathroom, pushing open the door and nothing. No sign of Reese. I look under the bed and even in the closets, not that I expected to find her there, but fuck me, I was hoping she was just playing some kind of trick on me.

No trick.

She's gone.

Heading back to the bathroom, I take care of business before searching for my phone. I find it on the nightstand next to the bed. Grabbing it, I have no missed messages or calls. I open the messaging app and send Reese a text.

Me: Where are you?

I wait. I count to one hundred and no reply. Fuck this. I dial her number, placing the phone to my ear. It rings four times before she picks up. "Hi," she says softly.

Just hearing her voice soothes my worry. "Where are you, babe?"

"Cooper," she sighs.

"Where are you, Reese?" Fear clogs my throat. Did she change her mind? Did she go back to him? No. She wouldn't do that. Not after what we shared last night. It was life-changing, to be inside her, to have her naked body in my arms while we slept.

"I think you need some time. We both need some time," she adds.

"Time for what? I don't understand. Tell me what's going on." I don't know what she's talking about, but I can guarantee I don't like it.

Time.

If she means time away from her, she's wrong, I've done that. I barely survived. What I need is her. Just Reese.

"I need some time, Cooper."

"How much time?" I manage to ask over the lump in my throat. She's pushing me away, and I don't know how to stop her.

"I don't know. I just… have a lot to work out in my head."

"About us? Reese, I love you. Let me help. Whatever it is, I can help," I say, pleading with her.

"Coop." She sniffs.

Fuck me. Now I've made her cry. "Where are you? I'll come to you." I stand and begin getting dressed as best as I can with one hand.

"No, Coop. I just need time. There is so much to process and think about. Yesterday I walked out of my wedding and last night… with you. I just need some time."

Shit. I sit down on the edge of the bed and run my free hand through my hair. I know she's right. I know she needs to take the time to work through whatever it is she has in her head, but damn it, I want to be the one to help her. I hate I'm part of the problem, that I'm an issue she potentially has to work out.

"Reese, last night meant everything to me. I meant what I said. I love you. I will always love you. You're it for me. For now and for forever. I'll give you some space, but please, baby, don't shut me out."

I hear a sob on the other end of the phone. "Thank you."

"How long?" I ask, knowing I'm pushing my luck.

"I don't know, Cooper."

"Where are you now?"

"I'm- taking a few days."

"What do you mean?"

"I mean that I'm not in town. At least, I won't be in about fifteen minutes."

"Where are you going?"

"I'd rather not say."

"You can't just go out of town and not tell me where you're going, Reese." She can't do this. She can't shut me out like this.

"I can, Cooper. I am," she adds. "I just need some space and time to think. A lot has happened, and I need to process it all."

"What if something happens? How will I get to you? At least tell me where you're going." I don't like the thought of her traveling alone. In fact, I fucking hate it.

"I can't. I know you, Coop. You'll come after me, and that's not what I need right now."

"I need you," I tell her. "In my life, by my side, in my bed. I need you, Reese. Please don't push me away," I plead with her. I know I don't really have the right to ask because I pushed her away first, but I apologized, and she knows how I feel about her. She's not once told me how she feels about me, about all of this.

"I have to go."

"No, wait," I rush to say.

"Coop," she says on a sob.

Even through the line, I can hear the anguish in her voice. "I love you, Reese. Not just for last night but forever. Nothing is going to change that. Not time, not distance. Nothing. You hear me?" She's quiet, except for a few sniffles. "Tell me you hear me, Reese."

"I hear you," she whispers.

"Will you call me when you get wherever it is that you're going? Will you call me while you're gone? Fuck, I just got you back, Reese. I can't stand the thought of being without you."

"I'll let you know that I made it."

"I love you."

"I need to go. Bye, Coop," she says, and the line goes silent.

Just like that, the bliss of having her in my arms, of us finally being together, is ripped out from under me and is replaced with fear. I was prepared for her decision to marry Hunter. I was prepared to lose her, but after last night… after what we shared, losing her isn't an option. Grabbing my clothes, I get dressed, and as I'm slipping on my shoes, there's a knock at the door. I rush, thinking maybe she changed her mind. I pull it open to find Nixon standing there with a bag and two coffees.

"Hey." I open the door, allowing him space to walk into the room.

"You look like shit." He places the bag and the coffees down on the small table, pulling up a chair.

"Yeah, well, when you fall asleep with the love of your life in your arms only to wake up to an empty bed and a phone call telling you she's going out of town and won't tell you where, that happens."

"I know. She has my fiancée with her."

"Tessa's with her? She didn't tell me that." I feel a little of the tension in my shoulders release knowing she's not alone.

"Yeah, you piss your girl off or scare her away or whatever the fuck happened between the two of you, and she runs off with my fiancée, so thanks for that," he says sarcastically.

"I didn't piss her off or scare her away. Not that I'm aware of. Fuck, man, I don't really know. When we went to bed last night, we were in a good place. I thought we were on the same page."

"That, my friend, is what you get for thinking." He points at me, along with an accusing look on his face.

"I don't even know what she was wearing."

"Clothes?" he offers.

"Yeah, but I kind of tore her dress last night." I more than just tore her dress. I tore it off her body. Not just a rip, it's ruined. There is no way she could have worn it out of this room.

He raises his eyebrows, a smirk on his face. "Oh, do tell."

"No. But I will tell you she wouldn't have been able to wear it out of here." I shrug because I'm not the least bit sorry about it.

"She texted Tess to bring her some clothes at around five this morning."

"I'm glad." The thought of her traipsing around in a robe from the hotel or worse, those thin pieces of lace, sets my blood on fire. Reese Latham is for my eyes only.

His phone rings, and I freeze, eavesdropping on him as he answers. "Hey, babe." He listens and smiles. "I love you too. Call me when you land," he says, then hits End on his phone.

"Where are they?"

"I'm not allowed to tell you."

"Why the hell not?" I ask, frustrated. She already told me she didn't want me to know, but damn it, she's the love of my life. I should know where she is.

"We all know you, Reeves. What's worse is we all know you when it comes to Reese. You're the dumbass who just figured it out."

"What's that supposed to mean?"

"I've been telling you for years that you were in love with her. Go ahead, say it. I was right."

"You were right." I don't even hesitate because I am in love with her. I have no plans of ever denying that truth ever again.

"Hold up." He grabs his phone from the table, hits a few buttons, and points it at me. "All right, say it again. A little louder for those in the back," he jokes.

"Fuck off." I laugh at his antics. "What did you mean, you know how I am when it comes to Reese?"

He takes a swig of his coffee before answering. "You've always been protective of her. Not just 'she's my best friend' protective, but 'I love this girl, and you're not getting near her' protective."

I don't reply to that, because I know deep down he's right. Reese has always been special to me. "So what? I'm just supposed to sit around and worry about her while she's gone?"

"She's fine, Cooper. Do you really think I would be okay with Tessa being in any kind of danger? If something happens, which it's not going to, I'll let you know."

"Thanks." I run my fingers through my hair and let out a slow, choppy breath. It's going to be a long… hell, I don't even know how long she's going to be gone. I assume she had time off work for her honeymoon, but I don't know where they were going. No, as soon as I got the wedding invitation, I made sure to sidestep any wedding talk. I couldn't bear it.

All I can do is hope she comes back to me. That we have our chance once and for all, to see where life takes us. Together. Not as best friends, but as lovers, and as life partners, and if I'm lucky, husband and wife.

That's my end goal.

I'll wait as long as it takes. I'm in for the fight of my life, and I'm ready for battle. I've never wanted anything or anyone like I want her. Whatever it takes, I'm ready.

Chapter 4

REESE

Sliding my phone back into my purse, I smile at Tessa. She's been my savior in all of this. I don't know what I would have done if she hadn't rescued me. Not just at the banquet hall but this morning as well. My dress was shredded, and in no way was I able to wear it. Call me crazy, but I'm not much for walking around fancy hotels in my underwear.

"How did it go?" she asks.

"Like I expected it to go. He's convinced we're meant to be together, at least for now. I don't think all this has sunk in for him yet. He's upset I won't tell him where I'm going. Oh, and he loves me," I say flippantly, but it's my heart that does the actual flipping each time he says those three little words.

"How does that make you feel?" Tessa asks.

I turn to look at her, and she has the most serious look on her face that has me busting out laughing. "What are you? A therapist?" I laugh.

"Yours, yes. Now, answer the question," she says, fighting a grin of her own.

"I love him, Tess. I always have, and I know I always will."

"But?"

"But... this is what he does. He's never wanted to see me with anyone else. He hated that I was dating Hunter. It had nothing do to with Hunter himself. We all know he's a great guy. That makes it even worse. I just left him there. Standing in front of our family and friends as I ran with my tail between my legs."

"I know it seems harsh, but just think about if you would have gone through with it. You didn't want to marry him, Reese. Doing so under false pretenses would have been worse than leaving him at the altar. Especially since he was waiting for marriage."

"I know," I sigh, tilting my head back against the seat and close my eyes. I don't know how I let things get so screwed up. "It's not that I didn't love Hunter," I say. "It's that I didn't love him enough. Not the way I should. You know?" I peek an eye open to find Tess watching me.

"Now boarding Flight 9874 to Mexico," the announcer calls over the PA system.

"I'm going to call Nix really quick before we board." I watch as she pulls out her phone and makes the call. It's short and sweet. She tells him we're getting ready to board and that she loves him. "Ready?" she asks, sliding her phone back into her purse.

"Yes."

"Thank God for travel insurance," she quips, standing and picking up her carry-on. "I'm excited it's my first time out of the country."

"Mine too."

"Are you disappointed that you're missing Hollywood?" she asks.

"Not even a little bit. That was all Hunter. He wanted to see the Hollywood sign, and shop on Rodeo Drive."

"It was your honeymoon too, you know?"

"I know. When he brought it up, he was so excited I didn't have the heart to tell him no."

"You know what I think?"

"What's that?" I ask, taking another step forward in the boarding line.

"I think that you knew deep down it's not what you wanted. I think that Cooper coming to you was the best possible outcome. Regardless of how things turn out for the two of you, I think your decision to walk away was the right one. That's why you let him make all of the decisions. That wedding wasn't you, Reese. Not one single factor, other than you being there, had any of you in it. Your heart and soul weren't into it."

"Miss," the attendant calls for my attention. I step forward and hand her my ticket and passport. She does her thing and sends me on through. I step forward and wait on Tessa to join me.

Once we're in our seats, and our carry-ons are put away overhead, I turn to look at her. "How did I let it all get so out of control, Tess?"

"Do you want me to answer honestly or tell you what's going to make you feel better?"

"Both?" I say, then immediately reply with, "Honestly."

"You love him. It's as simple as that, and by him, I mean Cooper. For years you secretly held onto hope that the two of you would one day be together. You can't just turn it off, Reese. No matter how hard you try, you just can't. I think Hunter was... *is,*" she corrects, "a nice guy. He was safe and comfortable, and he was there when Cooper wasn't."

"Oh, God." I cover my face with my hands. "I'm such a terrible person."

"No, you're not. However, you're going to have to talk to Hunter and Cooper eventually. We can't hide out in Mexico forever. I have a wedding to finish planning, and I intend to be there from start to finish." She leans into me, a smile playing at her lips.

"I'm happy for you. You and Nix have it all together. Talk about relationship goals."

"Honestly, you could have the same thing. You kind of already do with Cooper. Sure, it's been a bumpy road getting to this point, but you both love one another. It all hinges on if you want to make it work."

"I know he loves me. We've been in each other's lives since we were kids." He loves me, but the jury is still out on if he is truly in love with me. There's a big difference between the two.

"It's more than that."

"Is it? Why, all of a sudden, is it okay to jeopardize our friendship when it wasn't a year ago? Okay, it's been longer than a year, but you get my point. Why now?"

"I have my suspicions, Reese. However, I'm not the one you need to be asking these questions to. It's Cooper. He's the only one who can give you the answers."

"A week from now, he'll realize it was a mistake. All of it. The confessions of love… last night. By the time we're back home, he's going to have realized his misstep." Tessa mutters something under her breath that sounds like stubborn. I open my mouth to ask her, but the flight attendant begins her speech.

Once we're up in the air, we both decide a nap will do us some good. It takes me a while to fall asleep, but when I do, it's no surprise that it's Cooper I see in my dreams.

Mexico is beautiful. When our plane landed, there was a limo driver holding up Tessa's name. She immediately called Nixon, and he told her that since she and I were only planning a spa day the week of their wedding, she could consider this her bachelorette party.

"I mean, it's not really a party if it's just the two of us," I tell her as we're sipping our fruity alcoholic drinks on the beach outside our villa. Yes, villa. Nixon went all out.

"It's all the party I need. It's more than I wanted, but I have to admit. A week with my bestie on the beach before embarking on married life is just what the doctor ordered."

"Look at us. Me running from marriage and you running toward it."

"I wouldn't say you're running from marriage. You're simply changing lanes. Whether you're ready to admit it or not, we both know Cooper is where your heart has always been. If I'm being honest, I'm excited to see how this plays out."

"What?" I turn to look at her.

"You're in denial. The two of you have switched roles. For years you held out hope that the two of you would be together, as lovers and as friends. Now, he's on board, and you're worried he's lost his mind." She laughs. "It's going to be fun."

"I'm glad my life amuses you."

"Oh, it does," she says teasingly. "I've been around for the Cooper and Reese show for years. I've been rooting for the two of you. Hell, we all have. Now, it's time for the two of you to cheer for yourselves. It's time for you to decide what you want and allow your heart to accept that you can have the man of your dreams."

"What did they put in that drink?" I ask. "You know as well as I do he's going to regret this."

"What is *this* exactly?" She smirks. "I still don't know why you needed clothes or how that dress of yours got ruined."

My face heats, and it's not from the hot sun beating down on us. "Things got... interesting."

"Interesting as in you finally slept together?" It's not a question she needs the answer to. I'm sure my flaming blush of embarrassment is answer enough. "It's been five long years of foreplay that we've all been sitting front and center for. I'm kind of disappointed I didn't get to see the grand finale."

"Tess!" I scold, and she throws her head back in laughter.

"You're not denying it." She points a long, manicured finger at me and takes another sip of her fruity alcohol.

"He ripped it off me," I confess.

"Seriously?" she asks.

"Yep."

"That's fucking hot, Reese. It's all that pent-up sexual tension the two of you have been passing back and forth over the years."

"He just didn't want it to be Hunter."

"You're right, and you're wrong," she tells me. "He doesn't want you with Hunter because he loves you."

"You don't know that."

"Actually, I do know that."

"How?" I'm sure it's just her suspicion, but maybe, just maybe whatever she has to say will help me work all this out in my head.

"He told me."

"What do you mean, he told you?"

"The day of the rehearsal. Nix and I found him sitting in the parking lot waging a war with himself on whether or not he could go inside. Nix called him out on his feelings for you, and he told us he loved you."

"Because of the wedding. You know as well as I do that Cooper has always been protective when it comes to me, to a fault. Like my father, he thinks that no man will ever be good enough for me."

"Yeah, but your dad was willing to give you away. Cooper, on the other hand, was not."

"He didn't protest. He had the chance. He was there in the back row and didn't say a peep when the preacher asked if anyone objected."

"What would you have done if he did that, Reese? How would you have acted?"

"I don't know."

"Did you want him to stand up and declare his love for you?" Her voice is soft.

"Is that so bad? He comes to me and says he loves me… not just that he loves me, but he's *in* love with me. It's done behind closed doors. That night in his room at the house, that was behind closed doors, even though he pushed me away. Last night was again behind closed doors. He says he wants me, yet it's all words, Tessa. I want to believe him. My heart is screaming at me to believe him. My head, well, that's another story." I pause and finish off my drink. "My head tells me the facts. That I've loved him for years, and when I offered him more, he refused. Now, all of a sudden, when I'm set to be married and live happily ever after, he wants me. Tell me that doesn't sound like he just wants something he can't have?"

We're both quiet as we stare out at the ocean. I want to believe he loves me. I want to believe we can ride off into the sunset, but I know that if I let myself think that way, if I let my heart wrap around his, that when he decides to push me away again, I will never survive it. I know this. I know my heart can't take thinking he's mine and losing him all over again.

"I hear what you're saying and agree with you. Although, I know it's different this time. I see it in him, in both of you. It's easy for me to say this as an outsider looking in."

"I don't know where to go from here, Tess. I'm at a loss with how to move forward. My heart and my head are at battle, and I don't know what to do." My voice cracks as the emotions I've been trying to hide shine through.

"It's simple," she says, finishing off her own drink.

"Oh, yeah? Care to enlighten me?"

"You make him work for it."

"What?"

"You heard me. Make him work for it. You're worried he's going to change his mind. You're worried he's only telling you he's in love with you because he doesn't want to lose your friendship. So make him show you. It's more than just the words; it's also the actions."

"I get what you're saying, but how do I do that?"

"Tell him the truth. That you want him, that your heart wants him, but you're scared. Leave the ball in his court. See what he does."

"I don't know if I can do that and still not get crushed."

"Let me ask you this. If the two of you don't end up together, romantically, do you still want him in your life?"

"Yes."

"Then you have to find a way. You have to look past the fear and the hurt, and you have to give it a shot. I know you, Reese. I know he is the only man you want. You have to take a risk."

"Take it slow," I say, repeating her earlier words.

"Yep," she says, popping the *p*. "Tell him your fears. The only way any relationship is going to work is with honesty. You never told him how bad he hurt you, and he never told you how pushing you away hurt him."

"I know we need to sit down and talk."

"And let him woo you." She grins. "See just how serious he is. Sure, you kept the fact that he hurt you to yourself, but you offered yourself to him, and he refused. He needs to prove he's ready for more."

"Do I tell him that?"

"No. Tell him the truth. The pain you've been hiding and that you want to take things slow. See how he acts. If your theory of him wanting what he can't have is true, he'll get bored. If he loves you, like I know he does, he's going to show you."

"You sound pretty confident."

She shrugs. "I am. Like I said, I'm an outsider looking in. I can see past the issues to form my own opinion. I'm right, by the way. In case you were wondering."

"I hope so," I say softly, just as my phone rings. I reach for it on the towel beside me and show her the screen.

"How many times is that today?"

"I've lost count."

"He's worried. You should answer him."

I nod and hit Accept on the call, placing the phone to my ear. "Hello."

"I miss you." His deep voice washes over me.

"It's been a day," I counter, but I can't help the way his words cause my heart to race.

"A day too long. You having fun?"

"Tess and I are on the beach." It's the first hint I've given him since our conversation yesterday at the airport.

"I can hear the waves."

"Yeah. It's peaceful. Nix said we can call this Tessa's bachelorette party."

"Is she not having one?"

"This is it."

"Thanks for texting me to let me know that you made it there okay."

"You're welcome."

"Can you do me one more favor while you're there, wherever there is?" he asks.

"What's that?"

"Don't let another man steal you away from me before I've had the chance to fight for you."

His words cause my belly to flip. "Is that what you're going to do?"

"Yes." There is no hesitation, only absolute certainty, in his voice.

"Okay."

"*Okay* you won't let someone else take you away from me or okay I'm going to fight for you?"

"Both."

He exhales loudly. "Good. I'll let you get back to what you were doing. I just wanted to hear your voice. If you change your mind about me being there, let me know. I can be on the next flight out."

"You don't know where I am."

"It doesn't matter. I'd be there." We're both quiet for several heartbeats. "I love you, Reese. Tell Tess I said hello."

"I will."

"Bye, baby."

"Bye," I say, and hit End on the call.

"Well?" Tessa asks.

I relay my brief conversation to her, and she smirks. "Told you so."

"We'll see." I say the words, but inside, I'm screaming that I want her to be right. I want Cooper to fight for me. For us. I want to see this is more to him, that he really does love me. Not just the thought of me, or the me he thinks he can't have. I want him to love all of me. One thing's for sure. Tessa's right. Only time will tell. I need to give him the chance to prove it to me and still hold on to the few shreds of my heart that are remaining.

Chapter 5

COOPER

Tossing my phone on the bed, I stare up at the ceiling of my childhood room. I left for college five years ago, and it still looks the same as the day I left. I wonder when Mom is going to change it? I checked out of the hotel yesterday, and this is where I ended up. Nixon and I hung out for a couple of hours before he decided he was going home to Louisiana. He offered for me to go with him, but I knew that both my parents and Reese's had questions. I owed them answers.

It was late when I got in, I texted my parents that I was headed their way, and they left the front porch light on for me, just like they did when I was a kid. Using my key, I snuck inside a little before midnight and went straight to my old room. I've been hiding here ever since. I've been up since six, and I've called Reese a few times. Okay, more than a few since then. I'm surprised she answered. I needed to hear her voice. Not just that, but I needed her to know I'm going to fight for us. I've done nothing but think since I woke up in that hotel room all alone, and it's a feeling I never want again.

I know Reese better than she knows herself, and I understand she's scared. I meant what I told her, that I'm going to fight for her. For us. Whatever it takes for her to be by my side, I'll do it. Tossing the covers off me, I stand. It's after ten. It's time for me to face the music. Grabbing some clothes, I take a quick shower, and head downstairs.

"Morning, sleepyhead," Mom says from her seat on the couch.

"Morning." I take a seat next to her. Resting my elbows on my knees, I rub my hands over my face. I have no idea how this is going to go, but I have to do it.

"Rough night?" Dad chuckles.

I lift my head to look at him. "Rough year."

"Tell us all about it."

"I will. However, I think Eve and Garrett need to hear it too. Do you know what they're up to today?"

"No, but we can call them." Dad reaches into the pocket of his jeans and pulls out his phone. "You want them to come over?"

"Yes."

"Wait." Mom holds her hand up, and Dad stops what he's doing. "Tell us what this is about."

"Reese."

"Is she okay?" Mom asks. There is true concern in her voice. She loves Reese like her own. They both do. If I have my say about it, she will be mine, ours, a part of this family for the rest of her life.

"I'm in love with her." I blurt the words, needing to get the truth off my chest. The room is silent as my eyes dart between my parents. "Say something."

They look at each other and at the same time say, "We know."

"What do you mean, we know?" I ask.

"We've known for years. It wasn't our place to interfere, so we kept it to ourselves," Mom explains.

"Son, it was something you needed to realize on your own. You needed to feel it here," he says, laying his hand over his chest.

"Everyone keeps saying they knew," I mutter under my breath, causing them both to laugh.

"I take it you have something to do with Reese running out on her wedding yesterday?" Mom asks gently.

I nod. "I told her that I'm in love with her at the rehearsal."

Dad whistles. "Talk about timing."

"Yeah. Anyway, I know Garrett and Eve have questions, and I feel as though I owe them answers."

"Does Reese know you're going to talk to her parents?"

"No. She's… out of town with Tessa." Mom nods, which tells me she already knew.

"You know what? I'm just going to go over there." I stand and wipe my sweaty palms on my jeans.

"What exactly are you going over there for?" Dad asks.

"I need to explain why she walked out, that should fall on me. I'm the one who dropped this on her the day before her wedding."

"Reese is her own person, Cooper. You didn't make her walk out of that banquet hall," Mom says gently.

"No. You're right. I didn't make her, but I'm damn glad she did. I think they need to know that as well." Dad nods, and Mom has a small smile tilting her lips.

"We're proud of you, Cooper."

"For destroying a wedding?" I ask.

"No. For following your heart."

"I love her. I'm going to fight for her." It feels good to say it aloud.

"Show her, son. That's all you can do is show her," Dad says.

"That's the plan." I give them a wave before heading out the front door and across the yard to Reese's parents' place. I march up the steps and knock on the door, not giving myself the chance to change my mind.

"Cooper," Eve says, opening the door. "We didn't know you were home. Come on in." She pulls the door open wider. "You know you don't have to knock. You're always welcome here." She smiles warmly. "We just had a late breakfast. Are you hungry?" she offers.

I'm starving but didn't come over here to eat. "No, thank you," I say politely, following her into the living room.

"Look who I found," she tells Garrett.

"Cooper, good to see you. How long are you in town?"

"A while," I say vaguely. I don't want to leave until she's home and I have a chance to see her. Hell, I don't want to leave her at all. Technically

I don't have to. I have a few engagements with the team I have to go back for, but it's a three-hour drive, so that's manageable.

"Not that we're not happy to see you, but what brings you by? I'm sure you know that Reese isn't here. She and Tessa went to Mexico for a week," Eve says, not knowing that I didn't know where she was.

"Yeah, I knew they were out of town." I don't bother to tell her she just spilled the beans. "I actually wanted to talk to the two of you."

"Oh, what's going on?" Eve asks, her motherly concern shining through.

Here goes nothing. "I'm the reason she ran."

They both stare at me with blank expressions.

"I'm the reason Reese walked out on her wedding, and I'm so sorry. I'll repay you for everything—" I start when Garrett holds his hand up to stop me.

"There will be no talk of you paying for anything."

"Cooper, you didn't make Reese change her mind. Furthermore, we're not upset that she did. All we want is for her to be happy. We'd much rather her walk away now than live a life of misery or go through a nasty divorce later," Eve explains.

"It was me though. I saw her at the rehearsal dinner. I passed you in the hall, remember?" I ask Eve, and she nods. "I went to her and told her I was in love with her. I begged her not to go through with it."

A slow smile crosses Eve's face as she looks over at Garrett. "She's been waiting since the day we moved in, and you and Reese hit it off, for you to say those words." Garrett chuckles.

"That's my mistake too. I was blinded by our friendship. I didn't want that to change, but it did anyway. I was losing my best friend regardless, so I thought it was time to tell her how I felt. This past year, being away from her, it's been hell," I admit.

"So, what are you going to do?" Garrett asks. "What are your intentions with my daughter?" He grins cheekily. "I've always wanted to say that."

The fact he's making jokes has relief washing over me. "Did you not say that to Hunter?" I ask, barely able to say his name. He did nothing wrong, but in my eyes, he's still the enemy.

"No. Hunter didn't talk to us before he asked Reese to marry him."

What a douche. "I love her." My voice is steady and calm. "I want to spend the rest of my life showing her. I hope I have your blessing." It's not a question.

"And if you don't?"

"I'm going to love her anyway. That's what she deserves. Nothing less."

"Of course you have our blessing." Eve reaches over and lightly smacks Garrett on the arm. "He's messing with you, Cooper. We've always known the two of you had deep-rooted feelings for each other."

"My parents said the same thing. Why didn't I see it sooner?" I ask myself out loud.

"You did," Eve assures me. "But the fear of losing your best friend kept you from naming it and letting it grow. The separation did the two of you some good."

"Yeah, except she ran to another country."

"Oh, hush." Eve waves her arm in the air. "She just needed some time to get her head together and work it all out. You know Reese. She's a thinker. This is what she does."

"I'm glad Tessa is with her."

"We are too. I was relieved when she told us."

"So, what now?" Garrett asks.

"I don't know. I'm going to stay here until she comes home from Mexico, and then take it day by day. I love her." I look him in the eye when I say this. "I love her, and I'm going to fight for her. I've pushed her away for years." I gloss over the hottest night of my life in college, that was up until our night together in the hotel. "I'm going to show her what she means to me."

"You sound determined," he observes.

"I am."

"I'm afraid you're going to have your work cut out for you," Eve chimes in. "She's loved you for years, Cooper. She was sure there would never be anything between the two of you. I don't know what happened to make her think that. Give her some time, and please don't give up on her."

"Never." The conviction in my voice is unmistakable.

We spend the next hour catching up on life. Garrett and I talk about my first year of playing in the league, and Eve asks about living in Indy. I've missed them. They were such a huge part of my life growing up. It's been nice to catch up. I just wish Reese could have been here too.

"I should get back." I stand. "For what it's worth, I'm sorry. I never meant for it to turn out this way, but I'm glad that it did. Watching her walk down the aisle to him… it broke me. I never want to feel that way again." They don't say anything, and they don't need to. I said what I needed to say. The looks on their faces tell me more than words can.

They're rooting for us.

Walking back to my parents' place, I feel as though a weight has been lifted off my shoulders. Our families know where I stand. Now I have to decide which course of action to take. How am I going to prove to her that she's all I want?

Making my way into the house, I find it's quiet. Mom left a note on the counter telling me that there are leftovers in the fridge and that she and Dad ran to the hardware store. Grabbing the plate from the fridge, I pop it in the microwave and pull my phone out of my pocket. There is a two-hour time difference in Mexico, which means that Reese and Tessa were on the beach bright and early this morning. She's always loved the ocean. I wish I could be there with her. I decide to send her a text.

> **Me:** Hey. Just had a visit with your parents. I told them you calling the wedding off was my fault.

Her reply is immediate.

> **Reese:** It wasn't your fault, Cooper. I just realized I wanted something different.
>
> **Me:** Does that something rhyme with Trooper?
>
> **Reese:** You're impossible.

She follows her message with a line of laughing emojis. It's not a confession of love, but it's not a denial of one either.

> **Me:** Enjoy Mexico. Stay safe.

I follow it up with some hearts. My emoji game is on point.

> **Reese:** Damn it. Cooper, please don't come here. I need some time.

Her words sting a little, because all I want to do is be with her. All the time. However, I know she needs this time to work out what's going on in her head. Just like her mom said, Reese is a thinker, and a lot has happened in a very short amount of time.

> **Me:** I won't. Not unless you need me. I love you, Reese.

> **Reese:** Thank you.

The microwave dings, and I pull out my plate of food, taking it to the living room. I turn the television to the sports network that's talking about the upcoming draft. I get lost in the sport I love, all the while still thinking about Reese and the possibilities of our future.

REESE

I'm on my flight back to Ohio. Tessa and I said our goodbyes at the airport as she's flying home to Louisiana. I already miss her.

I'm so grateful she was able to come with me this week. It was nice to just catch up and talk about her wedding, while trying to forget about mine. There's a churning in my gut for what I did. How I acted. I was unsure after hearing Cooper's confession. However, if I'm honest, the doubts were there long before Cooper ever confessed he loved me. I just didn't know how to handle it. I'd let it go too far. Hunter is a great guy. He didn't deserve to be treated that way. I should have been upfront and honest with him.

I need to talk to him. That's something I was able to work out while I was in Mexico. He deserves to hear from me. It's going to be a hard conversation, but it needs to happen. Hell, I'm not even sure he'll talk to me. I might have to get creative, but he deserves an apology. I'm following my heart, but in the process, I trampled all over his. That's not okay. I don't expect him to ever forgive me, but it's important he knows I will forever be sorry for the way I treated him. For the way I hurt him.

As for Cooper, I still don't know what to do.

I love him. I've always loved him. I just don't know if I can trust his declaration of love. I know he loves me, and he's never lied to me. I'm just worried about him changing his mind about what kind of love he has for me. Tessa told me all week I was being irrational. That I need to give him a chance to prove it to me. She's convinced he loves me.

I want him to love me.

Closing my eyes, I rest my head back against the seat. I've tried to read this entire flight, and I keep reading the same line over and over again. There's no use in trying. Eyes closed, the first thing I see is Cooper. The way he hovered over me. The look in his eyes when he entered me for the first time, and when he told me he loved me. I want so badly to believe him. I want to jump right into this with him, full-speed ahead, but I know that's not the best way to handle this.

Tessa said to let him woo me, and although I'm not sold on the wooing, I do feel like we need to take things slow. We could easily get swept up in one another from our history alone. I don't want that. I let us take things too far that night in the hotel room. We should have talked, and nothing else. Maybe then I might not be so conflicted as to how to proceed. When I told him I needed him, I meant it.

Looking back, I'll never forget that night, but I feel as though we need to take a few steps back. Ease into this… whatever *this* is.

The rest of the flight is spent reliving that night we spent together just one short week ago over and over in my head. My imagination all these years has nothing on the real thing. No matter what happens between us, I have that night. It's one I will always cherish.

I'm walking through the airport with my carry-on wheeling behind me when I hear my name called. I stop and look around but don't see anyone I know, so I keep walking.

"Reese!" I hear it again, and this time, I know the voice.

Cooper.

Following the sound, I turn to my right, and there he is. Standing tall, with a Defenders hat pulled down over his eyes. My breath hitches at the sight of him. He appears to be bigger than life with his arms crossed over his chest, his muscles on full display and his face, well it's lit up with a smile all for me.

Slowly, I make my way toward him. He drops his arms to his sides, and as soon as I'm within reaching distance, he snakes an arm around my waist and pulls me into his chest. His face is buried in my neck, and his grip is tight. No matter how hard I try, I can't resist wrapping my arms around him and hugging him back.

"I missed you," he says softly.

I pull out of his hold and realize we're causing a scene. He might have thought pulling the hat down low was a big enough disguise, but he was wrong. People are watching with their phones pointed our way. "We're being watched," I say under my breath.

"I don't care. Let them look."

"Cooper, people are going to talk."

"I don't care."

"You don't need a scandal," I remind him.

"How is this a scandal? I'm picking the woman I love up at the airport. They can kiss my ass if they don't like it. There is no scandal here."

"Until they find out what I did."

"What did you do?"

"The wedding."

"You didn't break the law, Reese."

"I know that. It was a week ago. I still need to apologize to Hunter."

Something flashes in his eyes when I mention Hunter. "I'm not hiding, Reese. I told you that."

"Fine, can we please get out of here?" I keep my eyes on him, not willing to make eye contact with anyone else. I can feel the stares as more and more people begin to take notice.

"That I can do." He laces his fingers through mine, and together, hand in hand, we make our way through the airport. Pointing fingers, and even more cell phones, are aimed in our direction. They don't know about the wedding, but it's only going to take one nosey reporter to do some digging to figure it out. I need to call Hunter before that happens.

We reach Cooper's Truck, and he opens the door for me. "Nice ride," I tell him.

"Thank you." He waits for me to be buckled in before closing the door and racing around to the other side. Once he's in, he leans on the center console, his eyes on me. "You know why I like this truck?"

"I'm going to take a wild guess and say it's not gas mileage."

He leans in close. "The tinted windows," he says before pressing his lips to mine.

I try to fight it. I hold still for as long as I can, but when his tongue swipes across my bottom lip, I know I'm in trouble. I kiss him back for the briefest amount of time before coming to my senses and pulling away.

"I missed you," he says again, his eyes hooded.

"We should go." I shift in my seat to face forward.

"Where are we headed? Your house or your parents'?"

Here goes. "My place. But I can drive. My car is at Mom and Dad's. If you can just drop me off there."

"I'll drive you."

"Then I won't have my car."

"You can use my truck."

"How long are you planning on staying?"

"I don't have to report to training camp until the end of July."

My mouth falls open. "You're staying here until then?"

"Yep."

"You can't do that."

"Yes, I can. I have a couple of prior engagements with the team, but I won't be gone longer than a day or two. Maybe you can go with me. I can finally show you my place."

"Where are you staying?"

"With you."

"Cooper. We can't do this. We can't jump into this like we've been dating for years."

"We kind of have."

"No. We were best friends. There is so much we need to talk about. You can't stay with me, Coop."

"I'll rent a place or stay in a hotel. I'll figure it out. All I know is that I'm not leaving Columbus. I want as much time with you as I can get."

"We need to talk."

"We will."

"I want my car."

"Okay." He nods, not taking his eyes off the road. "I'll take you to your parents' to get your car."

"Thank you." That was easier than I thought it would be. Cooper is stubborn as hell, and I know how he gets once he sets his mind on something. Impossible pretty much sums it up.

He reaches over and laces his fingers through mine. "How was your trip?" he asks again, keeping his eyes on the road.

I stare down at our joined hands. I know I should let go, tell him that this is too much too soon, but maybe I can bask in his touch just this time, during the drive to my parents.' I've missed him. Not just since I've been in Mexico, but this past year and before, if I'm honest. That night he pushed me away, created a divide. I know I'm just as much to blame for not being truthful. Maybe all of this could have been avoided.

"Reese?" he asks, glancing over.

"It was good. Great actually. I've missed Tessa, and I enjoyed getting to catch up with her. She caught me up on everything with their wedding, and helped me forget about mine."

"You didn't forget," he says gently. "I know you, Reese. I know you're tearing yourself up inside over this. I'm the one you should blame, not yourself."

"Actually, I should thank you."

"Thank me?" he says, surprised.

"I had my doubts," I confess. "I wasn't sure that marrying Hunter was what I really wanted. I didn't voice it because I was ashamed. He's a really great guy. He was good to me."

"I'm glad. I feel for him too, but at the same time, I'm so fucking grateful that I have this chance with you. To show you what you mean to me."

I don't say anything to that. I'm not sure if I'm ready to have this conversation in his truck as we travel down the highway. When we get to my place, because I know he's going to follow me home, we'll talk. And while I don't want to push him away, I want us to ease into whatever this might be. Maybe, just maybe, I can keep my heart from falling even more in love with him in the process.

Four hours later, we're pulling into my building. Mom and Dad were chatty, and so were Cooper's parents. None of them seemed surprised we were together or when Cooper took my hand to lead me out to my car.

Cooper insists on carrying my bag as I let us into my apartment. "I'm going to grab a quick shower. Wash the travel off me. Make yourself at home."

"Need any help?" he asks, taking a seat on the couch. He already knows what my answer is going to be.

"I think I can manage. I'll be right back."

Rushing down the hall to my room, I strip out of my clothes and take the world's fastest shower. Pulling on some leggings and an old Central University T-shirt, I brush out my hair and quickly blow it dry. No styling for this girl. I'm in for the night. Instead, I pull it up in a ponytail and call it good.

"That was fast," Cooper says when I take a seat opposite him on the couch.

"I can take fast showers."

"That's a new skill," he jokes.

"Hush." I toss a pillow at him, and he catches it easily.

"You ready for that talk?" he asks.

"No. But we have to anyway." I've put it off as long as I can.

"You want to start, or do you want me to?"

"I will." I need to get this out. "For this to work, whatever this is, we need honesty. In order for that to happen, we need to backtrack."

"This is forever, and we can go back as far as you want." He angles his body toward mine from his spot on the couch.

I nod, pull the pillow back from his arms into mine as a safety net, and start talking. "I don't know when exactly that I fell in love with you." His eyes light up. "Only that I did. One day you were just Cooper, my best friend, and the next, you were the man I wanted more than anything. I wanted you as my best friend, and my everything."

He doesn't speak but reaches over and places his hand on my leg. We're now fully facing each other from opposite ends of the couch.

"I never wanted to tell you. I don't know if it was the fear of rejection or the fear of losing you that scared me more." I pause, collecting my thoughts. "Anyway, that night, the one where things got a little out of control in your room… that night I wanted you. I offered myself to you, and you didn't want me."

"I did," he says. "I wanted you, but I was afraid to lose you."

I want to believe him. I want to push all of this out of my mind, but I can't stop now. I have to get this out. "My heart was broken, Cooper. Shattered tiny shards of glass splintered. It was hard for me to be around you, the pain of knowing you didn't want me that way was crushing." He opens his mouth to speak, but I raise my hand to stop him. "Hunter was there. He was a really nice guy. He was patient with me, never pressuring me for anything. I found myself spending more and more time with him. All of my friends were your friends. I couldn't escape you, unless I was with Hunter."

My heart hurts speaking those words. For me, for Cooper, and for Hunter. He's innocent in all of this. He gave me his heart, and I accepted it even when I wasn't ready to. He wasn't who I wanted, and I let him think that he was. I pretended he was, and that is unforgivable.

"Fuck," he mutters.

"The more time I spent with him, the closer we became. He's a good guy, Coop. He didn't deserve what I did to him."

"I'm sorry. I know my timing was terrible. I didn't plan to lay my heart out at your feet that day. I was going to just deal with it. I had lost you, and it was all on me. The minute I pulled into the parking lot that night, I knew that wasn't going to be possible. I sat out in my truck for longer than I care to admit until Nix and Tess knocked on my window. They could see it all over my face and encouraged me to tell you how I really felt. It was like them telling me to talk to you was the validation that I wasn't crazy. It was a sign I hadn't lost my mind, and this pain in my gut at the thought of you marrying anyone but me was real. So real, in fact, it had consumed me for weeks. I rushed into the building. I had to find you, and when I did, well, you know what happens from there."

"Yeah. I remember." I've replayed that night and the one following it more times than I can count. I wish I knew the answer. I wish this was easy. I want to be able to look past all the pain, to believe what he's telling me. To trust in this connection we've always had.

Bliss | 53

Chapter 7

COOPER

"I meant every word of what I said to you that night, Reese. I admit it's somewhat of a haze, but I know I told you I was in love with you. I also know I pleaded with you not to marry him. I take the fault in that. I'm sorry you're hurting, baby. I am. I wish I could take that away from you. What I'm not sorry for is you calling off the wedding. We wouldn't be here right now if you hadn't, and there is nowhere else I'd rather be." I look into those big green eyes as I say the words. Willing her to believe me.

"How are you so sure about this, Coop? I mean, you told me yourself we couldn't be more. Now you're telling me that I'm all you want. That's confusing. My heart is still back in your bedroom at the house when you told me we could only be friends. It's hard for it to get past that night and believe what you're saying."

"I understand that. I know we have a lot to work through, but, Reese, there is no one else I'd rather be in this situation with. I'm going to show you how much I love you. I know I need to give you more than just my words, and I plan to do so." She has no idea of the depths I'll go to. Whatever I have to do to prove to her that this is real, I'll do it.

She's quiet, staring off into the distance. I wish I could read her mind. If I could only know what she was thinking, I could ease her fears. I could help her with this. Hell, if she could only read mine, her doubts would vanish just like that.

"Talk to me."

"I need to see Hunter."

My shoulders stiffen, and my heart stalls in my chest. "What do you mean you need to see him?"

"I need to apologize."

Every single cell in my body wants me to protest. I want to tell her that she can't see him. However, I can't do that. She's right. He's innocent in all of this and deserves to have the questions, which I'm sure he has, answered. "Do you want me to go with you?" I offer. Part of me wants her to say yes, and the other part wants her to say no. I don't want to see her with him. It's not just Hunter; it's any man who's not me.

"I don't think that's such a great idea."

"Yeah, probably not, but if you wanted me there, I would be there." Anxiety creeps in as I worry about what he will say or do. Will she change her mind about this? About us?

She nods. "He might not want to talk to me or see me. I just feel like I owe him that much. He didn't do anything wrong."

"Have you heard from him?"

"No. Not a phone call or a text. Nothing. I know he's hurt, and what I did was wrong. I ran from him, and I ran from you." She pauses, taking a deep breath. "I'm sorry for skipping out on you. My heart just needed a break."

"I love your heart." It's true. She's such a caring, loving person. I'm so damn lucky to have her in my life. She's torn about how she walked out on Hunter, even though she knows it was the best decision for her. Hell, she's apologizing for skipping out on me at the hotel. While I was upset she wasn't there when I woke up that morning, I understood her needing time to get her thoughts together. Walking out of your wedding and making love to your best friend on the same day is a lot to take on and process. I get that.

She smiles, and it lights up my fucking world. "I never stopped loving you, Cooper. Not for a single second. I don't know what this is." She waves a hand between us. "But I want to find out. I'm so scared you're going to realize that your fear of losing your best friend is what brought all these emotions on. I'm scared I'm going to lose you. Lose you as my best friend, and as the love of my life." A single tear slides over her cheek.

I slide over next to her and caress her cheek with my thumb, wiping away the trail from her tear. "That's not going to happen, baby. I know that." I want to lean in and kiss her. Show her she's who I want, but now is not the time for that. "Now it's my job to show you."

"I want so badly to tell you we can't do this, but in equal parts, I want you to be mine." Another tear falls, and then another.

"Don't be scared, Reese. I've got you." I smile, trying to lighten the mood and stop her tears. "It's my fault. I made you think I didn't want you, and honestly, I was in denial. I wanted you that night. More than I've ever wanted anything in my life, but I was afraid of losing you. I'm not afraid anymore." I know this is our chance. Sure, in the back of my mind there's a nagging feeling telling me if this doesn't work out, things will never be the same. I just have to keep reminding myself that they haven't been the same since last year. It might not be Hunter, and if it's not me, it will be someone else. This is our time, and I'm going to fight for us.

"You don't know that. Things change. People change."

"There is one certainty in my life, Reese, and that's you. It's always been you. I compared everyone to you. There is no substitute for the real thing."

"Where do we go from here?" she asks, her voice small.

"Tell me what you want. Tell me how you see this playing out." Dropping my hand to her leg, I wait patiently for her answer.

"I'm afraid to say it out loud."

My thumb glides back and forth over her thigh. "It's just me. You can tell me anything."

"I want so badly for this all to work out. I want us to be together, but I really think we need to go slow. I want us to take our time, and even though we know everything about one another, I think we should start off as if we were strangers."

She'll never be a stranger to me. "What does that mean exactly?" I ask.

"We date. We don't jump into bed with one another, and we take our time with this new development in our relationship. I'm worried this is going to wear off for you. This is the only way I know how to keep my heart from being mangled if that's how this ends." I'm not a player. She knows that. That still doesn't keep me from being cautious about this. My intention isn't to play or lead her on. However, her fear is that I'm suddenly going to realize she's not what I want. The thought of losing me that has us in this position and not the love I'm declaring that is alive and well. I don't know why she just can't let go of this fear.

"It's not going to end."

"I really don't want it to," she confesses. "I just think that we need to take the time to build this new part of our relationship. Does that make sense?"

"It does. So we date," I say, not really loving the idea. I want us to be more permanent, but I'll take what I can get.

She nods, a slow smile pulling at her lips. "We date."

"Exclusively."

"Coop, maybe we should see how it goes?" she suggests.

"No. I want exclusivity. I don't want anyone else, and I don't want you seeing anyone else either. I want us both to be all in."

"That's… not what I was expecting." I hate that she's putting us both through this. I hate that she can't accept my word. I've never lied to her before. We've wanted this for so long. For us to be together like I'm offering. Her fear… it comes from having everything she's ever wanted, and then it being stripped away from her. I know that I crushed her. Now I just have to prove to her that will never happen again. Prove to her that my love for her is real.

"Good." I lean in and kiss the corner of her mouth.

"We just said slow," she reminds me.

"What? Slow means no kissing?"

"Do you usually kiss on the first date?"

"My first date experience is limited at best. Yours?"

"Limited, but I can tell you with Hunter—" She winces. "Never mind."

"No. Tell me. I need to hear it." I don't want to hear it, but I need to. Hearing her talk about the two of them will only fuel me to fight harder. A reminder of what I have and what I could have lost.

"It doesn't matter. What matters is how we do this."

"We start by you confirming that you're my girlfriend." I'm not a fool. I'm locking this shit down now. I don't want her to have any confusion or insecurities moving forward. "We said exclusive," I remind her.

"But that's dating exclusively. Do we have to label it?"

"Yes."

"Cooper, we said we were going to take our time."

"We will." I'm quick to assure her.

"No labels, not yet. I don't think jumping in headfirst is a good idea."

The look in her eyes tells me she's still carrying a load of worry on her shoulders. I want to argue with her, but pushing her away again is something I said I would never do, even from something like this. I can give her some time to get her head wrapped around the idea. Then I'm not going to take no for an answer. By then, she will see what she means to me. I won't stop until she does.

"For now," I concede. "We won't label it for now."

"Good." She holds her hand over her mouth to cover her yawn.

"I'm sure you're exhausted from traveling and then the drive here from your parents' place. You ready for bed?" I ask.

"Yes." She stands from the couch, leaving the pillow she's been clutching behind. "Where are you staying?"

"Here."

"You can't stay here, Cooper."

"Just tonight. It's late, and I just need to be here with you. I promise I'll be on my best behavior." I wink as I stand and stretch my arms over my head. "Reese," I say when her eyes travel to my waist where my shirt has ridden up.

"Tonight," she agrees. I bite down on my lip to fight the grin at this small victory. "I'll grab some blankets." She turns and walks away and takes my glee with her. At least I'm still here with her. I might not be in her bed, but I'm in her home. Small steps to get to the ultimate reward.

Reese.

"The spare room is still empty from when Tess moved out. I'll take the couch. You're too tall. You won't get any sleep."

"Nope. This is perfect." I take the blankets and pillow from her and lean over to kiss her cheek. "Night, baby," I whisper.

"Night, Coop."

She hesitates before turning to make her way to her room. I watch her until she disappears down the hall. I'm not looking forward to a night on the couch, but it's a small concession to be here with her. I've lived the last year without her. I don't want to do that ever again. I have three months before training camp. It's time to show the woman I love what she means to me.

Chapter 8

REESE

I'm wide awake, staring into the darkness of my bedroom. I've been lying here for well over an hour, unable to fall asleep. How can I when I know Cooper is in the other room? Any other time he'd be sleeping next to me. When my bedroom door opens, I quickly shut my eyes. He's quiet as a mouse as he steps into my room. I lie still, waiting to see what he does. He makes his way around the bed, something he's used to. He stayed here a lot back in college.

I feel the bed dip with his weight as he climbs in beside me. I'm frozen as I feel his body move close to mine. He wraps his strong arms around me and sighs at the same time as I take a deep breath. "I just need to hold you. I can't stand the thought of you sleeping in here without me." His voice is low and deep as he whispers in my ear.

I don't say a word as I savor the feeling of being in his arms. This is more than just a friend cuddling with a friend, something we did a lot in college. Looking back, I realize that's not really what friends do.

"I love you so damn much, Reese." His voice cracks and I bite my lip to fight my own emotions. "I'm sorry it's taken me so long to realize what was right in front of me." He's quiet for several long minutes. "I want to build a life with you. I can't think of anything better than spending my life with my best friend. I know you want to go slow, and I promise you I will try to respect that." Another long pause. "I want this moment, this very thing every night. I want to fall asleep with you in my arms and wake up to see those big green eyes. You are what I want, Reese."

Not able to resist, I turn in his arms. It's dark in my room, so I can't see him, but I feel his hot breath as it brushes across my face. His hand lands on my hip, pulling me to his chest. "We said slow," I murmur.

"You said slow," he replies softly.

"Coop," I breathe.

"Just let me hold you, baby."

His softly spoken request in the middle of the night is impossible to resist. Resting my head against his chest, I can feel his heart beating. His arms are locked tight around me, and it's perfect. It's everything I ever imagined it could be, and I don't know how I'm going to be able to resist him. I don't know what I was thinking. How could I possibly believe I could keep my heart safe? It's never been safe when it comes to Cooper. I gave my heart to him years ago, and he still has it. He will always have it.

"I missed you, Reese. So fucking much. I was starting to wonder if there would ever be a time I would get to have you all to myself again."

I pull away, but he doesn't let me get far, sliding his arm under my head and letting me use him as a pillow. "Tell me about football."

"What do you want to know?"

"Everything. I feel so disconnected from your life."

"This last year was hard. Painfully hard. I knew I would miss you, but I never could have imagined the depth of that void. I never want to go through that again. I can't do it. I won't survive it."

"That's pretty dramatic," I say, teasing and trying to lighten the mood.

"I'm serious," he says, his voice strong. "I was miserable without you. It wasn't until I got your wedding invitation in the mail that I realized what an idiot I'd been. I had the most amazing woman right in front of me for years, and let my fear keep me from her."

"I was scared too."

"Not that night in my room. You were fearless offering yourself to me. I wish I could explain to you how hard it was for me to stop us that night. I was certain it would ruin our friendship, and I knew I needed you in my life. I was just too blinded by the fear to realize that we could be more than just best friends." He leans in and, somehow in the darkness, his lips find my forehead. "I didn't realize we could be everything," he says tenderly.

"I feel like I'm dreaming."

"Yeah?" he asks. "Good dream or nightmare?"

"The best dream," I confess.

"You're my dream."

I can't explain what his words do to me. It almost feels as though my body is melting into his as I relax into his hold. His words put me at ease and have my heart leaping from my chest.

"Football," I prompt.

"I like the team. The guys are great."

"Come on, Coop, you can do better than that."

"To be honest, I was in a haze most of the season. I went to practice and gave my all there and at games, but socially, I didn't do a lot. I had a few guys from the team over a few times, doing my part to fit in, but I spent most of my time in the gym. I was missing you like crazy, in a new city all alone, and I just threw myself into my job."

"It shows," I say, resting my hand on his chest.

"Don't tempt me, baby," he says, swatting my ass playfully. "What about you? How's work?"

"I like my job, but there is a lot of government red tape we have to go through. There's a lot I didn't get to see during my externship. I just want to help people. There was this woman… hell, she's my age. She came into the office. She's a nurse's aide and a single mom. The dad is not in the picture and gives her no financial support. Anyway, health insurance is expensive, her deductible is outrageous, and her son, who's four, has asthma. She was trying to get the medical card to help offset the deductible. She's struggling to buy his meds and make ends meet. I helped her submit for financial assistance, a medical card, anything to help lessen the burden. She made five dollars too much. Can you believe that? Five dollars kept her from getting the assistance she needed to keep her head above water. I hate it. It's so hard to tell them that news. I thought being a social worker, I was going to get to help people, help make a difference in their lives, and it's been the exact opposite so far."

"I'm sorry." He places another soft kiss on my forehead.

"Well, I'm glad one of us has our dream job."

"Maybe it's just working for the county. Are there other avenues, places you can work that you can feel more fulfilled?"

"Possibly. I like my coworkers. I'm just riding it out, getting some knowledge and experience under my belt for now."

"Maybe you can look for a new job," he suggests.

"I've thought about it a lot recently."

"Maybe you could look in Indy."

It's a casual suggestion, but the meaning behind it is nothing close to casual. "Maybe. Although adding the stress of finding a place to live and learning a new city doesn't sound appealing."

"You could live with me." He tightens his hold. "Just consider it, Reese. I hate the thought of being away from you. We could see each other every morning and every night."

"Do you know the definition of slow?" I ask him. I'm teasing. I know that he knows. I'm just trying to distract my heart as it thunders in my chest at his suggestion.

"Not when it comes to you. No."

"That's a big step."

I feel him nod. "It is, but at the same time, we're not strangers. Yeah, this is a new development in our relationship, but to hear everyone around us talk, they've been waiting on this and expecting it for years."

"Who?"

"My parents, your parents, our friends. Everyone says they saw this coming. I just wish they would have pointed it out to me sooner. Maybe I could have pulled my head out of my ass a long time ago."

"Did they tell you that? Our parents?" I ask. Although, I'm not surprised. My mother has dropped hints for years how she thought Cooper and I looked good together. I would roll my eyes, while inside I was secretly thrilled she thought so. Looks like I didn't hide my feelings as well as I thought I did.

"They did. Nixon too."

"Yeah, Tess said something similar while we were in Mexico." I guess it's not a bad thing we have so many people in our corner.

"I want this, Reese. I want you. I agreed I would try to go slow, but I need you to know that slowing this down doesn't change the way I feel about you. It doesn't change the fact you're all I think about, and the life I want with you is all I can see when I think about the future." He's quiet for a few minutes. "Every future has a past, Reese. This is our story. We choose the ending."

I'm certain he can feel the way my heart is racing. His words make me want to throw caution to the wind and jump in eyes closed, hoping for the best. I just need a little time, and I need to talk to Hunter, though. He really does deserve an apology.

"You're making this hard for me," I confess.

"Good. Because the thought of being away from you is tearing me up inside. This last year was pure hell, and I never want to go through that again."

I snuggle into his chest, needing to be close to him. "I missed you too, Cooper."

He doesn't reply, but the tight hold of his arms around me tells me everything. He's never been like this. We used to cuddle a lot, but this, needing me close, and not being able to stay away. That's all-new. It's new, and even so, my heart craves it. Not just my heart but me. I crave him. There's no doubt in my mind that Cooper is the man for me. And somehow, here in the darkness of my room, he's managed to chip away at my doubts that this is really what he wants.

I want him. I want this life he talks about, the two of us and happily ever after. I guess only time will tell what the future brings.

Chapter 9

COOPER

The morning sun gleams in through the window. I blink slowly, opening my eyes and adjusting to the light. A smile immediately breaks out when I see Reese is still in my arms, still facing me just as she was last night. I've woken up in her bed before, and her in mine, but this time it's different. This time she's going to wake up knowing she slept in the arms of the man who loves her.

Carefully, I push her hair out of her eyes, and they flutter open. "Good morning, beautiful," I say, leaning down and kissing the corner of her mouth.

"I need to brush my teeth," she mumbles.

"You're here in my arms. That's the last thing I'm worried about. How did you sleep?"

"Like a rock."

I want to puff out my chest at that. She slept like a rock in my arms. Mine. Where she belongs. "What's on the agenda for today?" I ask instead of gloating. I have a feeling that will get me nowhere.

"Toothbrush, shower, and food. In that order."

I chuckle at her. "What's after that?"

"I need to call Hunter."

I nod. "Are you surprised he hasn't reached out to you before now?"

"No. Not really. He's a good guy. He's never pressured me, and I know he's hurting."

"I'm sorry."

"Me too, but it's for the best. It might have been bad timing, but it's better in the long run. I mean, he was saving himself for his wife. I could have taken that from him. I know we would have made it work, and maybe in time, I would have been able to give him more of me, but… I don't think so."

"Why is that?" I ask. My heart hammers in my chest, waiting to hear her say it. I know the answer; it's me. Don't judge me. I need a small morsel of something when it comes to her.

"You."

It's not a confession of love, but I'll take it. "The offer still stands. If you want me to go with you."

"No. I need to do it on my own. Besides, that's kind of a slap in the face bringing you with me."

"Why? For all he knows, we're just friends." I'm sure by now he's heard rumors or even figured it out on his own. Nixon said it was written all over my face. It's also no coincidence I was the one that rushed out of the banquet hall after her.

"I think our friends and family have proved otherwise."

"You're right. I don't hate the guy, but he wasn't the man for you." I lean down and kiss the tip of her nose. "No one can love you like I can."

"Who are you and what have you done with my best friend?" she asks, a slow, sleepy smile playing at her lips.

"Didn't you hear? Your best friend fell in love," I say, and her eyes soften. "Now, go grab that shower and toothbrush you were rambling about, while I make us some breakfast."

"I'm not sure what our options are. I guess I should add going to the store to my list of things to do today," she says, climbing out of bed.

"We can do that."

"We?"

I nod. "Yes, we. Now go." I walk toward her and snake my arms around her waist before she can get away. I give her a hug and kiss her neck softly before releasing her. I leave her to grab her shower while I rummage through her cabinets.

She's right. She has nothing. There's a small diner just down the street we used to frequent in college. After a quick search, I have their number, and I call in an order. I should be back just as she's finished getting ready. Not wanting to find me gone and think I ran, I head back down the hall and knock on the bathroom door.

"Yeah," she calls out over the running water.

I push open the door and curse the fact she has a dark green shower curtain. "Hey, babe, I'm going to run to the diner and grab us some breakfast. You were right. The kitchen is bare. You need anything else?" *You know, like help with that shower?*

"Told you. No, I'm good. Thanks, Coop," she calls back.

Reluctantly, I close the bathroom door, grab the keys from the kitchen counter, and lock up behind me. I walk since it's just a block over, and call Nixon on my way.

"Where should I send the bail money?" is his greeting.

"What the fuck? What makes you think I need bail money?" I ask.

"Because I know your stubborn ass, and Reese sent Tess a message telling her you were waiting at the airport for her. I know your stubborn ass too well and assumed Reese had to call the cops to get you to leave." I can hear the humor in his voice.

"For your information, I stayed at her place last night."

"Really?" He's surprised.

"Yes, but nothing happened. We talked a lot, and then I might have got fed up with the couch and crawled into bed with her," I confess.

"How'd that go over?"

"She didn't kick me out. We talked some more, and I woke up this morning with her in my arms, where she's supposed to be."

"You know, I'm kind of glad you didn't realize you were in love with her until now," he tells me.

"Why's that?" I'm almost afraid to ask.

Bliss | 69

"Because I would have had to listen to all this sappy 'I'm in love' bullshit all four years of college."

"Like I didn't listen to you when it came to Tessa."

"Dude, you don't hear yourself. You've got it bad." He laughs.

"Yeah, I do. I'm not ashamed to admit it. I also know what it's like to not have her in my life, not fully. When you experience that, you'll learn to cherish what you have and shout it from the rooftops too."

"You think I don't cherish my fiancée?" he asks, surprised.

"No, I know you love her. I just mean that until you know what life is like without that person, you won't get it. You and Tessa are solid, have been since day one. Be grateful for that. I was the dumbass who pushed Reese away. Then, I was the same dumbass who found out what life is like without her. It changes you. At least it did me. I want anyone and everyone to know how I feel about her."

"Tess, babe!" I hear him call out.

"Yeah?" she asks.

"Cooper loves Reese."

I can hear Tessa's loud laugh through the phone. "This isn't new news," she tells him.

"Did you hear that?" Nixon asks me.

"Yeah, I heard her." I'm not sure where he's going with this.

"So, you see, you might think you need to tell the world, but we already knew. Seems to me that you and Reese are the only two who didn't get the memo."

"Well played, my friend, well played," I say as I enter the restaurant. "Anyway, I need to go. I just got to the diner to pick up breakfast. Just wanted to check in."

"You two need to come and visit," he tells me.

"I'm not sure if Reese can get the time off work. I'll talk to her about it and let you know."

"We can go to them." I hear Tessa say in the background.

"If not, we'll come to you," he tells me.

He might not be as boastful about his fiancée, but I know damn well she's the love of his life. They have it together and are where I hope

Reese and I can one day be. One day soon. Sliding my phone into my pocket, I step up to the counter. "Order for Reeves," I tell the waitress.

"Oh my God, are you *the* Cooper Reeves?" she squeals.

"That's me," I reply awkwardly. I love my fans, but I just want our order so I can get back to Reese.

"What are you doing here? I mean, I know you went to college here, but what brings you back to town?" she asks, batting her eyelashes at me.

She looks not a day over eighteen, if that. No, thank you. I'm not interested. Not now, not ever. "My girlfriend lives here. And breakfast?" I hear myself saying. I fight back my grin at calling Reese my girlfriend. She's not there yet, but to me, that's what she is. In fact, she's more than that, but saying you're getting breakfast for the love of your life sounds weird, even to me. However, this girl doesn't seem to be getting the hint. I might have to use that line to get our food.

"Me and some friends are hanging out at the bar next door tonight. You should stop by." Again, she bats her eyelashes. They're fake as hell, and that's just not sexy. Not to me.

"No, thanks," I tell her flatly.

"Oh, come. It will be fun." She winks.

"I'll be spending the night in with my girlfriend, and since you didn't catch that the first time, let me break that down for you. I'm not interested. She's the love of my life. No bat of your eyes or any other offer you have is going to change that." I give her a hard look.

"Whatever," she quips. "Your loss."

"Not hardly," I say, not giving a fuck if she hears me. She rings up my order and hands it to me. I don't miss her writing her number on the back of my receipt before she drops it in the bag. Taking my card and sliding it back into my wallet, she smirks, handing me the bag. I reach in, pulling out the receipt and make a show of wadding it up. "Can you toss this for me? No point in bringing home more trash," I say, and turn to walk out.

I'm seething mad at the audacity of her, and not watching where I'm going, which is why I collide with someone. "Sorry," I say, looking up to see my victim, and I freeze. "Hunter."

"Cooper." He nods.

I don't have to ask him if he just heard my declaration. I can see it written all over his face. "I'm sorry, I—"

He raises his hand to stop me. "I don't want to hear it. Give Reese my best," he says, stepping around me.

I reach out and grab his arm. "She wants to see you."

"We don't always get what we want."

"Don't take this out on her." I plead her case.

"No, after your little speech, I concluded you were just as much to blame. Not that I didn't already know that."

"We didn't mean for this to happen."

"So, what? She runs out on me and now she's yours?" The anger and the hurt in his question are evident.

She's always been mine. "Not exactly," I say instead. "Just let her explain. Please."

"Yeah, we'll see. You better get that food to the love of your life. It's going to get cold." He turns and rushes down the hall to the restrooms.

I debate going after him, but I've caused a big enough scene as it is. People are staring. My only saving grace is that Hunter kept his voice down. No way could anyone hear our conversation. Not that they needed to. The tension was thick and obvious.

I rush out the door and start toward her place. When she hears this, she's going to be pissed. How was I supposed to know Hunter was going to be there? And the waitress, I told her I was taken, and she kept flapping her jaws about meeting up. I was over that shit and wanted to end it. I'd much rather today's event occur than it get back to Reese that I was entertaining the idea. Yeah, fuck that. It is what it is, and we'll deal with it. Together.

Chapter 10

REESE

When Cooper got back to my place yesterday and told me about his run-in with Hunter, my time was officially up. I knew before then, but I needed to reach out to him. It was way past time. I called him, but he didn't answer, and I had to leave a message. Four hours later, I sent him a text, and three hours after that, he finally replied. I was able to convince him to meet me. He chose his place. Today at six. Which is why I'm standing outside his apartment building, trying to garner up the courage to go inside.

My phone vibrates in my purse, and I'm grateful for the distraction. "Hey," I greet Cooper.

"Hey, babe. You almost there?"

He wasn't thrilled about me coming to see Hunter right after work. Something about too long a time without seeing me, but when he found out I was coming to Hunter's apartment, that complaint was thrown out the window as he tried to convince me to change it to a more central location. I get where he's coming from, but he doesn't know Hunter like I do.

He's a great guy, he would never hurt me. I'm the one who's been doing that all on my own. If he feels more comfortable at his place, that's what we'll do. It's a small concession after leaving him at the altar.

"Yeah. I'm standing outside his building. Did you find a place to stay?"

"About that," he says, and I already know what's coming. "Why can't I stay in your spare room? I promise you won't even know I'm here. I'll even buy a bed."

"Cooper, you are aware that you've snuck into my room in the middle of the night the last two nights?" Not that I'm complaining. I sleep better when his body is wrapped around mine. I have no willpower when it comes to him, and him ending up in my bed each night, even if nothing happens, is not really taking it slow.

"That's something we've done since we were kids," he counters.

"Yeah, but things have changed, Coop."

"Thank God for that," he says, and I can hear the smile in his voice.

"Can we talk about this when I get home?" Glancing at my watch, I see it's five minutes until six.

"Sure, I've got dinner covered. I'll be here waiting for you."

"I'll see you soon."

"Reese?"

"Yeah?"

"I love you. Never forget that. I know this is going to be hard for you, and I'm here. Whatever you need, I'm here."

I love you too. "Thanks, Coop," I say instead, and end the call, sliding my phone back into my purse.

My feet feel as though they are lead weights as I walk into the building and wait for the elevator. I've been dreading this, but it's the right thing to do. I hate that he ran into Cooper yesterday and heard him basically saying we are together, and everything is all hunky-dory. That's not the case. At least, not yet.

Stepping onto the elevator, I hit the button for the fourth floor, and watch as the numbers slowly climb. Thankfully, there aren't additional stops along the way. The door slides open, and it's with not only heavy feet but a heavy heart that I make my way to his apartment. Hunter's a great guy. He was always good to me. I'll never forgive myself for hurting him the way I did. I should have called it off a long time before we got to our wedding day. To be honest, I never should have said yes. He might not see it now. One day he will. One day he will find the true love of his life, who will give as much as he does, and he'll understand.

Reaching his door, I knock softly, tapping my fingers on the door three times, and then bow my head, waiting for him to answer. When he opens the door, I slowly lift my head. He's standing in the door, just staring at me. "Can I come in?" I ask, my voice weak.

He steps back and motions for me to enter. I make my way to the living room and sit on the couch. Not knowing where to look or what to do with my hands, I reach into my purse and pull out the key to this very apartment and place it on the table. "I thought you might want that back."

"Yeah," he replies, his voice gruff. "Uh, let me get my keys." He's back in no time at all, handing me the key to my place.

"Thanks," I say, taking it and dropping it into my purse. "Hunter, I'm so sorry." He doesn't say anything. He won't even look at me, so I forge ahead. "What I did was unacceptable. I was having doubts, and I should have talked to you. I don't expect you to ever be able to forgive me, but please know I am deeply sorry," I say, fighting back tears. The crack in my voice has him turning to look at me.

"I loved you. I still do," he says softly.

I nod. "I know. I love you too, but not enough. I know that sounds harsh, but you deserve someone to love you who has zero doubts, zero reservations."

"Why didn't you just talk to me? We could have postponed the wedding."

"Hunter," I say, biting my lip to keep the tears from falling. I take a minute to get my emotions in check and then try again. "I never would have been able to give you all of me. I thought that I could, but I know now I never would have. That's not fair to you."

"You told me that the two of you were just friends. That there was nothing between the two of you," he says accusingly.

"That wasn't a lie. Cooper and I were best friends, have been since we were kids. All of that is true. What I didn't tell you is that I've been in love with him for longer than I can remember." He flinches, but I know he needs to hear this as much as I need to say it. "In fact, I don't know when it happened. I just woke up one day, and he was more to me. I never told him. I never wanted it to tarnish our friendship. One night, in college, before you, there was kissing, and it ended in us saying we should just be friends."

He sits on the chair, silently listening as I tell him the reason I broke his heart. "So, there was something?" he finally says.

"For me, yes," I confess. "That night, the night he decided we couldn't take that leap of faith, my heart shattered. I loved him. I knew I had to move on. I had to forge full-steam ahead with my life and stop waiting around for him to feel the same way."

"So what, I was your rebound guy?" He winces as he says the words.

"No, but I guess when you think about it, maybe." My heart hurts at admitting this. "Hunter, I enjoyed my time with you. I do love you."

"Just not enough to marry me?"

"No. I'm sorry. I know that's hard to hear, and it's just as hard for me to say it, but it's the truth, and after what I did, you deserve the truth."

"Why not earlier that day? Huh? Why did you wait until we were standing there with everyone watching to tell me you couldn't go through with it?"

"I wasn't sure I wouldn't. I struggled with my decision. Trust me, it was not made lightly. I agreed to marry you. I gave you my word and didn't want to go back on that. However, I also owed it to myself and to you, to be honest. It wasn't until I was standing before you that it hit me that not only was I not being true to myself, but I wasn't being true to you. You deserved better, and that's what led me to walk away."

"And Cooper? What role does he play in all of this?" he asks.

I hesitate on what I should tell him. It feels like if I tell him about Cooper confessing his love for me at the rehearsal that I would just be digging the knife deeper into his heart. I don't want to hurt him anymore than I already have.

"I saw him, Reese. Did he tell you that? I saw him at the diner just down from your place. The waitress was hitting on him."

I nod. Cooper told me how it all went down. "He told me."

"He was pretty blunt about the fact he had a girlfriend that he was madly in love with. It was news to me he was dating, and then it hit me. You. He's in love with you. Did he tell you that too?"

I nod. "Yes."

"You still love him." It's not a question.

"Yes."

"Are the two of you together now? You go from my bed to his?" he asks hotly.

"Hunter, that's not fair, and you know it. Besides, we weren't sleeping together."

"You slept next to me, Reese. Here in my bed, in yours. We were committed to one another. You should have talked to me, damn it." He stands and runs his fingers through his hair as he begins to pace across the room. "You should have told me you were having second thoughts. We could have talked about it. We could have worked through it."

"There was no working through it, Hunter."

"Just like that. Over a year of our lives, just gone in a flash."

"Not gone. We still have those memories."

"Yeah, but they hurt, Reese. They hurt," he says flatly.

"I'm sorry." I wipe the tears from my eyes. "I know that nothing I say can or do will make this right."

"You're right," he agrees. He stops pacing and turns to look at me. "You can go now."

"Hunter, I—" I start, but he holds up his hand to stop me.

"I don't want to hear it, Reese. I don't know if I will ever be able to forgive you for what you did. You broke my heart."

I nod. I know I did, and I know how it feels, but I don't bother to tell him that. Besides, I don't think he would care. "I'm sorry."

"Goodbye, Reese. I hope you and Cooper are happy together." With that, he walks to the door and opens it. I've worn out my welcome.

Standing, I walk to the door and stop when I reach him. "I'm so sorry, Hunter." His jaw is clenched, and his stare is hard as he stares off into his apartment. I got to say what I came to say, and I knew it wouldn't be easy. I've never seen Hunter act like this before, but it's understandable. After what I did to him. "Take care of yourself," I whisper and walk out the door.

Thankfully, I don't have to wait long for the elevator, and the ride down is quiet as well. When I make it out onto the street, I pull in a deep breath, slowly exhaling. I hate that I hurt him, but it's what's right for both of us. We both deserve better. Him especially. He needs someone who will love him the way I love Cooper.

Cooper might have confessed his love to me, but I knew I didn't love Hunter, not the way he deserved to be loved. This is on me, and I take responsibility. Cooper said that every future has a past. I can only hope our pasts are entwined with our future. That we're able to navigate these rocky seas and find our way back to shore. I want that more than anything.

I'm barely in the apartment with the door shut behind me when Cooper engulfs me in a hug. I don't fight the connection; instead, I wrap my arms around him and hold on tight. This is exactly what I needed. We stand here for several long minutes before he finally releases his hold on me and steps back.

"Come sit." He takes my hand and leads us to the couch. He sits and pulls me into his lap. I'm about to object, but his words stop me. "I know slow, but I also know you need this. Let me hold you."

I relax into him, never able to resist being close to him. "It's been a long day."

"Want to talk about it?"

"Not really much to say. He's hurt and angry, as he should be. I hate that I hurt him."

"I know you do."

We're quiet for a few minutes. I think about the conversation with Hunter. Even though it was hard, it needed to happen. I also feel as though a weight has been lifted off my shoulders. He didn't have to let me in. He didn't have to give me the chance to say I'm sorry, but he did. My wish for him is that he finds love. I hope he finds someone who loves him as much as I love the man holding me in his arms right now.

"I made dinner," Cooper says softly. "Are you hungry?"

I lift my head from his shoulder to look at him. "You cooked? Or ordered takeout?" I raise my eyebrows in question.

"I cooked."

"Really? So what are we having?" I inquire.

"Spaghetti. Before you ask, yes, it's jar sauce, but I spruced it up with some hamburger, and I got those twisty bread roll things you love."

On impulse, I lean in and kiss his cheek. "Thanks, Coop."

"If that's the response I get, I need to take some cooking classes in the off-season." He grins.

"I'm starving, but I want to change out of these clothes." I stand from his lap and head to my room to change. Five minutes later, I find him in the kitchen setting two heaping plates of spaghetti on the table. "This smells delicious."

"Oh, it is," he assures me.

"How modest of you," I tease.

"All in a day's work," he says, pretending to brush off his shoulders.

"Sit, crazy man." I laugh.

"How did it go?" he asks, taking a huge bite of his dinner.

I finish chewing and wipe my mouth. "Like I expected it would. But it's the closure I think we both needed."

"Good," he says, taking another bite. "Damn, either this is good, or I'm starving."

"It's good. When did you learn to cook?"

"Living on your own, missing your best friend, tired as fuck from grueling games and practices. A man can only eat so much takeout."

"So, what else can you cook?" I ask.

"I make this rice dinner. It's more of a concoction, but it's really good. I just kind of toss things in. Spaghetti, grilled chicken, and steak, of course, on the grill. That's about it. I'm a work in progress."

"Well, you're doing great," I say before taking another bite.

"Thank you."

We eat our dinner with little tidbits of conversation here and there. The majority of the time, we're both stuffing our faces. I feel like I can't walk from the amount of food I consumed. Having had enough, I push my plate away from me. "I can't finish it all. It was delicious, but I can't eat another bite."

"I'm glad you liked it," he says, finishing off his last bite.

"How was your day?" I ask him. I'm fully aware of how domesticated this feels. Even more than that, is how right it feels. With him here.

"Good. I spent the morning on the phone with my agent going over my appearances. I also have a commercial I'm shooting in a couple of weeks."

"Really?"

"Yeah," he says, his cheeks turning pink. "It's for an insurance agency."

"I'm so proud of you, Coop."

"Thanks, babe." He reaches out and squeezes my hand lightly. "About my staying here," he says.

"I think we're going to need to get comfortable for this one," I say, standing and rinsing off my plate and putting it in the dishwasher. Cooper puts the cheese away while I take care of his plate and a few other dishes before we head to the living room.

"You have the space," he says, once we are both sitting facing one another on the couch.

"That's not the point, Coop. We're supposed to be taking this slow."

"I don't think you know how hard that is for me."

"Do you not think that this is hard for me? That's the reason I asked us to take some time with this. I was supposed to be marrying another man not even two weeks ago."

"I know that." His voice is low. "I don't need you to remind me you were supposed to be his. I don't need you to remind me this is my chance to show you what you mean to me. I can rent a place or stay in a hotel, but I only have a couple of months before I have to go back to Indy. To my job. I want to soak up as much time with you as I can between now and then. I only have a small window of time to show you what you mean to me. I want to be here, Reese. I promise you I will respect any boundaries that you put into place. Just… please let me be here with you."

I replay his plea over and over in my mind. He's right. He's going to be leaving, heading back to his life and his career. I don't know what's happening between us, but I do know that the more time I get to be with him, the harder it's going to be for me to let go. Knowing that, it doesn't stop me from saying, "Okay."

"Yeah?" He leans in close. "Thank you." He kisses me softly, a simple press of his lips to mine, maybe a couple of seconds, but it leaves me wanting more.

"Yes. But we will have boundaries."

"Anything." He grins.

I have a feeling the next several weeks are going to be an adventure.

Chapter 11

COOPER

I've been staying at Reese's apartment for two weeks. Two weeks of locking myself in the spare room at night, in a weak attempt to not sneak into her room and cuddle up with her. So far, I'm holding strong. It's been difficult, but I'm trying to respect her boundaries. This queen size bed seems larger than life without her lying next to me.

It's been two weeks of pure bliss, though. I don't know of any other way to describe it. One little word sums up the reality of my life. I love her more today than I did yesterday and even the day before. I'm confident I will love her even more tomorrow.

We have dinner together each night, and then lounge on the couch. We've spent a lot of time in, but that's fine by me. I know she's worried about running into Hunter while the wounds are still healing, and I understand. I know that's hard for her, and I don't mind keeping her to myself. Sure, I want the world to know she's mine, but right now, she's just that. All mine. I don't have to share my evenings or weekends with her with anyone else. I'm loving every minute of it.

This weekend, however, is a little different. Reese has an event for the county at the local children's home. She described it as a mini carnival for the kids. Local businesses donated prizes for the games. I know she's stressing over it being enough. She wants the kids to have a great time.

"How many kids are there?" I ask Reese. It's Saturday morning, and she's just finished getting ready to leave.

"Ten rowdy boys." She smiles.

"They're all boys? Is it an all-boys home?"

"No, it just happened to be that way. We never know who is going to be staying at the home at any given time. New kids come in at all hours of the day, and some are getting fostered and even sent back to their families."

"Is that a good idea? I mean, they were taken for a reason, right?"

"Yes. Some cases, yes, it's a very good thing. Then there are cases that it's not. It all depends on the reason they were removed from the home, and if that issue, whatever it might have been, has been resolved. It's mostly drugs that we're seeing."

"Damn, babe. I don't know how you do it."

"It's difficult, but I enjoy it. I just hate all the red tape. It's really heartbreaking when you see the same child in and out of the home because the parents or guardians can't seem to get it together."

"I bet." She's tough, but I know this gets to her. She's said several times over the last couple of weeks that she wishes she could do more. I dropped the hint she could look for a job in Indianapolis, closer to me. She kind of brushed off my suggestion. She might have forgotten or thought that I did, but I'm just buying my time to bring it up again.

"I need to get going." She drapes her purse over her shoulder and grabs her keys from the table. "What are you doing today?"

"I don't know yet." It's a lie. I know exactly what I'm doing today, but it's a surprise for her.

"All right. Well, this goes until midafternoon. So, I won't be home before then. I'll see you tonight?"

Is that hope I hear in her voice? "I'll be here." I stand and follow her to the door. "Have a good day, babe." Leaning in, I kiss her temple. "Love you." She doesn't say it back, but her eyes soften. I know she feels it. The love we share. She just needs a little more time to be convinced I'm not going anywhere.

I wait about ten minutes after she leaves to pull the boxes I've been hiding out of the closet. I called the public relations department of the Defenders and asked for some jerseys and other Defenders gear. I had them send some pink for the girls, but it looks like it's just my girl who's going to need that one. Her jersey was special order. I'll take it today, just in case. I was going to leave all the other pink jerseys here, but I think I'll just sign them too and leave them at the home for any future Little Miss Football Fans who might come through the doors.

I spend the next hour signing thirty jerseys, some foam footballs, and posters. Mary, the lady who handles the Defenders PR, also threw in some stickers and temporary tattoos. I rebox it all, and it doesn't fit as well as it did before I unpacked it. Shrugging, I leave the lid open, grab my keys, phone, and tap my back pocket to make sure I have my wallet. Thankfully, there is an elevator. I'm not about to try to break my neck carrying this big-ass box down the stairs to get to my truck.

Fifteen minutes later, I'm pulling into the parking lot of the children's home. I leave the box in the back seat for now as I go in search of Reese.

"Hi, can I help you?" a teenage girl asks. She's wearing a name tag that reads Sage and has *volunteer* written underneath it.

"Hi, Sage. I'm looking for Reese Latham."

"Sure, is she expecting you?" she asks, sounding way more grown up than she looks.

"She's not. I was kind of hoping to surprise her." I wink, and her face flushes.

"I-I'm not supposed to let just anyone in," she says with apology in her voice.

"Are you Cooper Reeves," a little boy asks, staring up at me.

He couldn't be older than nine or ten. I crouch down to his level. "I am. What's your name?"

"Travis. You're my favorite player," he says with awe.

"Thank you, Travis." I hold my hand out for him to shake, and he doesn't hesitate to slide his small, frail hand in mine. "It's nice to meet you."

"Are you here to foster?" he asks, his eyes wide.

Fuck, that's a kick to the balls. These kids, I don't know how Reese does this every day. "No, but I am here to help. I'm looking for my girlfriend, Reese."

Bliss | 85

If I thought his eyes were wide before, they're the size of saucers now. "You're Ms. Reese's boyfriend?" he asks.

I nod. "You think you could help me find her?" I ask him. His little head is bobbing up and down like crazy before I even get the question out. I look up at Sage. "Is that okay? I'm one of the good guys, I promise," I tell her.

"Cooper?" I hear from behind me, and I would recognize that voice anywhere. Turning, I see my girl standing there with a look of confusion on her face, but it does nothing to hide her slow smile. "What are you doing here?"

"I came to help."

"I—" She starts but stops when Travis pulls on her shirt. She immediately looks down, giving him all her attention.

"Ms. Reese. Is Cooper Reeves really your boyfriend?" he asks excitedly.

She glances up at me, and I shrug unapologetically. "Mr. Reeves and I have been friends since we were your age," she explains.

"That's so cool." He turns to look at me. "Can we throw the football?" he asks.

"Sure, buddy. Later. Right now, I need to help Ms. Reese." Mrs. Reeves sounds better, but we'll get to that. "I promise we'll toss the ball before I leave today."

"I gotta go tell the guys!" He jumps in excitement, and then he's gone, rushing into the building to find his friends.

"What are you doing here, Coop?" Reese asks again.

"I wanted to support you. I have some gifts for the kids in the truck."

"This is a big deal. Word is going to spread that you're here."

"Good. Maybe it will bring awareness to the event, and the home."

"He's going to tell them all that you're my boyfriend."

"Even better."

"Cooper, this is serious." She tries to give me a hard stare, but I can see through her to know she's only making a big deal over this because she's still worried I'm not sticking around.

"I agree. The world should know you're mine."

"Ms. Reese," Sage says hesitantly. "The dunking booth is here."

"Thank you, Sage. Can you please direct them to the backyard? There's a sign that says reserved for dunking booth."

"Okay." She nods, smiling. Her shoulders straighten a little as if she's honored that Reese is trusting her with the task.

"Cooper—" Reese starts, but I step closer and place my finger over her lips.

"I want to be here, baby. This is me supporting you. I'm going to run to my truck and get the box, then I want you to put me to work."

"What's in the box?"

"Defenders gear."

"Where did you get it?"

"I called the PR rep for the team, had her send it to me."

She nods and swallows hard. "Th—" She clears her throat. "They'll love that."

I lean in and press my lips to her forehead. "Not as much as I love you." I pull back and turn to head back toward my truck. I smile when I think about the man I am with her. I'm waxing poetic and spouting off sweet shit, but I can't seem to help myself when it comes to her. I vowed to never hold back with her again, and I'm not going to. I love her, so I'm going to tell her and show her every damn day.

She's waiting for me at the door when I get back from my truck. "Where do you want this?"

"How about we rally the kids together and give it to them now? Before everyone gets there. I have a feeling the boys are going to need some time to get used to the fact that we have a professional football player with us today."

"Nah, today I'm just Cooper, your boyfriend."

She rolls those beautiful green eyes and smiles. "Come on, Romeo." She laughs and opens the door for me.

Once we're both inside, I follow her down a long hall that leads to a huge room. Glancing around, there are several couches, a TV, a bookshelf filled with books, and a large dining table that has pencil holders, and notebooks in the center.

"This is the activity room," she says as another woman enters the room.

"Carla, this is Cooper Reeves. He brought some gifts for the kids."

Carla smiles politely, and I can tell she has no idea who I am. "That's very nice of you."

Reese chuckles. "Cooper is a running back for the Indianapolis Defenders," she explains.

"Oh." Carla's eyes widen. "How did you find out about today?" she asks.

"My—" I start, and Reese interrupts me. I smirk.

"Cooper and I grew up together."

"Well, thank you for being here. The boys are going to be thrilled," Carla tells me.

"I was thinking we should bring them in now, let the shock and thrill of Coop being here wear off. We still have two hours before the event starts."

"That's a great idea. I'll go round them up."

"Thanks, Carla," Reese says and turns to me. "Let's get this all sorted before they get in here. They're going to want all of your attention."

"Jealous?" I tease.

She laughs. I love the sound of it. "No."

"Ouch," I say, placing a hand to my chest, pretending to be wounded.

"Not of these kids. They deserve to feel like they are the center of attention today. That's the point of today, after all." She starts pulling items from the box. "Cooper, these are amazing. The boys are going to love them."

"There are some pink too. I wasn't sure how many boys and girls until this morning. I went ahead and signed them."

"They're perfect. Thank you." She reaches for the jersey that's in its own bag. "What's this?"

"Oh, that? Open it." I'm not sure how she's going to take this, but here goes nothing. I probably should have it at her place instead of bringing it here, but there is no going back now.

I watch as she pulls the jersey out and holds it up. "Turn it around," I tell her." She does, and I hear a small gasp. "You don't have to wear it if you don't want to, but I wanted you to have it."

"*Reeves's Girl,*" she reads from the back of the jersey.

"Has a nice ring to it, right?" I ask her.

"Cooper." She lowers the jersey and gives me a look that I can't quite explain.

"It's you! It's really you!" a young boy says, racing into the room.

I lean into Reese and whisper in her ear, "I love you." That's the best I've got for her. She needs to see it, and she needs to hear it.

"It's really me," I say, pulling back from her. "What's your name?"

One by one, the boys take turns, shaking my hand and telling me their names. Reese stands next to me and passes out all the goodies to each of them. The smiles on their faces, and hers, is a smile I will never forget.

I've never really thought of myself as much of a celebrity before, but today, seeing the looks on their faces, and their eyes light up, I vow to use this new-found fame for good. Sure, I was popular in college, but this… it's an all-new level. I could actually make a difference, and with Reese at my side, together, we could make a huge impact. It's something I need to think about, but definitely an avenue I want to pursue.

Five hours later, the mini carnival has been cleaned up, and the boys are still bouncing with energy. "Do they ever slow down?" I ask Carla.

"Nope. Many of them have never experienced anything like today, so their high is going to last for a while. And you—" Carla pauses to glance over at me. "You made their year by being here and being so good to them. Thank you for that."

"Thank Reese. I wouldn't be here without her."

She nods. "She's a huge asset to us."

"I'm glad that's not going unnoticed."

"Cooper!" one of the boys calls out. "Come toss with us."

"Duty calls," I say, standing to stretch my legs and join the boys where they're gathered just a few feet away. "All right, how about some drills. I'm going to toss each of you the ball, and you toss it back then go to the back of the line. That will get us all warmed up," I say, holding up my hands for the ball. Joey, one of the smaller boys, rears his arm back with all his might and tosses it to me. It doesn't even make it halfway. I hold in my laugh and move forward to retrieve the ball.

I spend the next twenty minutes or so letting them toss me the ball. "All right. We're going to mix it up a little. I'm going to yell *go,* and you take off running, but keep your eyes on me. I'm going to toss you the ball, and you're going to try and catch it. This works on your speed as well as your hand-eye coordination," I explain.

Pass after pass, the boys try their hardest to catch the ball. A few of them made it happen, and the others, the smaller of the group, came pretty close. There have been a lot of laughs, and today has reminded me why I love this game. I don't know how many nights after dinner my dad and I would do this very same thing. Then when we moved next to Reese, she and her dad would join us while our moms watched from the lawn chairs.

It feels as though every part of my life is entwined with hers, and I love it. I love *her* for it. She has been there when I was just a kid with big dreams, and now, today, she's here living that dream with me. At least I hope she will be.

"Boys!" Carla calls out. "It's time to come in and get cleaned up for dinner."

"Aw, do we have to?" one of them complains.

"Hey, now," I chime in. "You need to listen to Carla and the other adults. They're just looking out for what's best for you." There is some collective grumbling, but they nod as each one of them lines up to give me a high-five.

"You're good with them," Reese says, walking toward me.

"They're all good kids. I hate that they're here." I point to the large building.

"Yeah, me too. However, what's worse is that this place is better than where they were. This gives them structure, stability, a safe place to lay their head and food in their bellies," she says sadly.

"You're doing good work here, Reese."

She shrugs. "I'm their social worker. It's my job to look out for what's best for them."

"I agree, but you went above and beyond today. No one before you has ever taken their own time to plan something like this for them."

"You were a hit," she says, ignoring my compliment.

"We make a good team."

She smiles up at me. "Yeah, we really do."

Reaching out, I entangle my fingers with hers and lead her to her car. With a quick peck on the lips, I promise to see her at home.

Home.

Reese is my home.

Chapter 12

REESE

Reaching for my coffee cup, I find it empty. With a heavy sigh, I toss it into the trash can and debate on running out to grab another. I'm exhausted. It's been a long day. When my phone rang at four this morning, I knew it wouldn't be good. It never is in my line of work. Cassie, a little girl who just turned six, was removed from her home. This is the third time she's been removed, and this time there were signs of abuse.

I wasn't working for the county the first time she was removed, but I was there the second during my internship. Luckily, we were able to place her in foster care. Her parents did the required rehab, and she got to go home. This time, I don't know what's going to happen, but I have to wonder when is enough *enough?* When does the court system not see that this isn't what's best for her, to be bounced around?

I've been trying to place her in foster care all day, but I don't have any families who can take her on. Not yet. There are many who are in training, but there just are not enough foster families to love and care for these kids. It breaks my heart.

Glancing at the clock, I see it's already five o'clock. I've done all that

I can do today, and it's time to go home. I don't need more caffeine. I need sleep. Lots and lots of sleep. Saving the court document I was working on, I close down my computer, and instead of packing up and bringing work home with me, I leave it all here. I need a night without it. I just need… to decompress from the sadness of the day.

I work for the county, but my office is in the children's home. Normally, I go and say goodbye to all the kids, pass out some hugs. I know I'm breaking the cardinal rule to not get attached, but I can't seem to prevent it. It's not in me to not care about these kids. That's the huge part of my frustration with my job. I don't feel as though I'm making a difference. Instead, I feel like a hamster on a wheel, just going through the motions. Just like Cassie. This is her third time being pulled from her home. *Third* time. I know we want to keep families together, but is that really what's best for her if that's the kind of environment she's living in? I'm conflicted and disappointed in our system.

I'm unlocking my car when my phone rings. Stopping, I dig it out of my purse and see Cooper's face smiling at me. "Hey," I greet him, unlocking the car and tossing my purse into the passenger seat.

"How's your day going?"

"Don't ask."

"That bad?" he asks.

"Unfortunately." Not like it's news to him. He's texted me a few times today, checking on me, asking me if I needed him to bring me anything. "Just one of those days," I say, starting the car and blasting the air conditioning. It's hot as hell for May.

"I've got dinner covered, just text me when you're on your way home so I can put it in the oven."

"I just got in my car."

"Perfect. I'll put it in now. Drive safe. I'll see you when you get home."

"Yeah," I agree. "I'm on my way."

"Reese?"

"Yeah?"

"I love you," he says, and the line goes dead.

He didn't give me a chance to say it back. Not that I was going to.

Sure, I want to. It's getting harder and harder to not tell him, but I don't want to do it like this. On a day that's been complete shit. That's not how I want to remember it. He knows I never stopped loving him. I told him that. However, I've yet to say the words. I've been holding back when it comes to declaring that I love him. Saying I never stopped and saying the three words I know he longs to hear are two completely different things. I feel as though after all this time, it needs to be the right moment. A small blip of time in our universe he will never forget. He deserves that, after all my waiting and uncertainty.

Things have been good between us. He's been staying with me for over a month now and he's kept to his promise about sleeping in the spare room, now that we have a bed in there. That doesn't mean he doesn't take any and all opportunities to touch me. When we're making dinner, which we seem to do together more often than not, he finds subtle ways when we're sitting on the couch after dinner, rubbing my feet or playing with my hair, while I rest with my head in his lap. If there is a way, Cooper has found it.

Most nights, I rush to my room to keep from begging him to sleep with me. Our night in the hotel room constantly plays on my mind. It was explosive and intense. I can't help but wonder if that's us… how we will always be, or if it was the tension and the fear taking hold of us. I admit I've been tempted to find out, but I'm holding strong.

Last weekend when he came to the home and spent the day with me and the kids, his support meant everything to me. I admit I keep waiting for the other shoe to drop, but nothing's happening. Cooper has proven to be certain in his feelings for me, and I him. I've always known I was in love with him. The issue is finding the courage to speak those words aloud. To finally give voice to what my heart has always known.

Fifteen minutes later, I'm walking into my apartment, and something smells delicious. "Coop, I don't know what that is, but I'm about to eat all of it," I say, tossing my keys on the small entry table and letting my purse fall to the floor. Kicking off my heels, I go in search of my roommate.

"In here!" he calls out from the kitchen.

"What smells so good?"

"Tuna noodle casserole." He grins.

"Since when do you know how to make tuna noodle casserole?" I ask.

"Since today. I know you love my mom's, so I called her for the ingredients. We FaceTimed while I put it all together."

I don't really know what to say to that. His actions don't scream "I can't wait to run away from you." They tell another story. One that tells me he's in this with me this time. He's all in, and after the day I had today, the emotions of that conclusion are almost too much to bear. I can't speak, so instead, I walk to him and wrap my arms around his waist, burying my face in his chest.

He doesn't speak, and neither do I. We stand here in the middle of my kitchen, holding onto one another as if it's our last time. "Thank you," I finally whisper.

"For what?"

"Taking care of me."

He pulls back, places his index finger under my chin, and gently tilts so we're looking at one another. "Never thank me for taking care of you, Reese. You're the love of my life. I'm always going to be here. Good days, bad days, and all the days in between."

"I—" I start, then stop myself. I almost let those three little words slip. "I need to go change. I'll be right back."

"Wine?" he asks.

"Beer," I call over my shoulder, heading to my room. I hear him chuckle and say, "That's my girl," or something similar before I disappear into my room.

Opting for comfort, I put on one of his old T-shirts from college that I stole years ago. I throw my hair up and wash all the makeup off my face. I don't plan on going out for the rest of the night.

"Let's eat," I say, walking into the kitchen.

Cooper, who has his back to me, turns and his eyes scan my body. "Babe, you should go put some clothes on."

"Why? It's just us, and it's not like you haven't seen it all before."

"That's why." He swallows hard. "I promised I would keep my hands to myself."

"It's just an old T-shirt." I look down. "It comes to my knees. Nothing remotely sexy about this."

"Turn around," he says gruffly. I do as he asks. "Fuck," he mutters.

"What?"

"I was making sure I remembered the shirt, and I was right. It has my name on it."

"Yeah, this is the CU shirt you got freshman year." I still don't see what the big deal is. "I stole it, but you knew that already," I remind him.

"I don't know if I can explain it without it making me sound like a possessive jackass."

"Try me." Part of me wants him to be a possessive jackass. I've waited my entire life to evoke these kinds of feelings in him.

He sets both plates that he fixed for us on the counter and stalks toward me. He doesn't stop until he reaches me and lifts me from my feet, setting me on the opposite side of the counter in my small kitchen. I brace my hands on his shoulders to steady myself as he steps between my legs.

His hands are braced on either side of me, gripping the counter. "I don't know that I have the words, but it's sexy as fuck. To see you in nothing but my shirt, my last name scrawled across your back." His eyes are heated as he stares at me.

"You've seen me like this before." I squirm on the counter to quell the ache that's burning inside me for him.

"I know," he says, his voice gruff with need. "Every fucking time I had to stalk off and take a cold shower. This is the first time since you've been mine that I've seen you in it."

"I'm not yours," I whisper the words but with zero sincerity.

"You are mine." He leans in closer, pressing a kiss to the corner of my mouth. His lips trail across my cheek and down my neck.

My body has a mind of its own, and my neck tilts to the left, giving him better access. I should be ashamed, but the feel of his lips and his hot breath against my skin is more than I can resist.

His hands grip my hips as he pulls me to the edge of the counter. His hard length hitting right where I want him. "Coop." I moan his name as the memories of what it felt like to have him inside me flash in my mind. My legs wrap around his waist as I try to get him closer. His cock is nestled between my thighs with nothing but his shorts and my panties separating us. I'm ready to throw caution to the wind and beg him to take me to bed when the shrill ringing of his cell phone interrupts us.

"Let it ring," he mumbles, his lips trailing back up my neck. "Nothing is more important than this," he whispers, his hot breath ghosting across my ear.

His phone stops ringing, and mine starts from where I left it in the entryway. "Coop," I say, dropping my legs from his waist. "It might be important."

"You're important," he says, kissing the corner of my mouth before pulling away. Reaching out, he grabs his phone. "It was my mom." There's a worried expression on his face when he taps the screen to call her back. He's still standing between my legs. He has one arm wrapped around me, while the other holds the phone that he puts on speaker so I can hear.

"Hello, my son," Ann greets cheerily.

"What's up?"

"Oh, I was just calling Reese since I couldn't get a hold of you," she says. Cooper looks at me and rolls his eyes.

"Is everything okay?"

"Of course, why do you ask?"

He looks at me and shakes his head. "What's up?"

"Oh, I wanted to see what you and Reese are doing for Memorial Day weekend?"

"We haven't talked about it."

"Well, we're having a barbecue. You two should come home."

He looks at me, and I shrug and nod. "Sure, we'll be there."

"Oh, good. I'll call Eve and let her know you're coming. Will the two of you be staying here or at their place?" she asks.

"Mom, I told you. We're taking it slow."

"Right. Of course, we'll both have the beds made up just in case. Tell Reese I said hello. We can't wait to see you," she says and ends the call.

"Told you it wasn't important."

"You did, but what if it would have been?" I counter.

He leans in and kisses my neck just as my belly growls. He chuckles and pulls back. "Grab us a couple of beers, and I'll heat up our plates." This time his lips land on my forehead before he grips my hips and lifts me from the counter. My legs are weak as I walk to the fridge and pull out two bottles of water. Tonight proves I have no willpower when it comes to him. We don't need alcohol to cloud our judgment. If he's on his best behavior, it's difficult, but I seem to manage just fine. However, when he's like he was tonight, my power to resist him is nonexistent.

Chapter 13

COOPER

"Are you ready for this?" I ask Reese as we hit the city limit sign for the town we grew up in.

"I'm not sure." She chuckles. "I know we've told them that we're taking this slow, but our mothers don't seem to understand that concept."

"It wouldn't surprise me if they have our wedding all planned out." I laugh.

"Really?" she asks, glancing over at me. "You're okay with that?"

"Sure. I mean, it doesn't bother me. We'll do it our way regardless of what they want. Let them have their fun." I keep my eyes on the road, but I can feel her stare.

"Cooper, you do realize we're talking about marriage, right?" she questions.

"Not just marriage, baby. Marriage to you." I reach over and link my fingers with hers. She doesn't pull away, not that I expected her to. I've been pushing the limits since that night in the kitchen. She's yet to stop me or push me away. I'm slowly wearing her down. I'm taking note of every one of my small victories.

"Hey," I say to get her out of her head. "What do you say we hit up Bill's Billiards tonight?"

"You up for a night of signing autographs?" she teases.

"Pfft, this is my hometown. I'm just some guy who grew up here." Sure, there's going to be a few of my old buddies reach out, but none of the fanfare that Reese is imagining.

"If you believe that, I have some oceanfront property just down from Mom and Dad's that I'll sell you."

"Are you going to live there with me? If so, you found yourself a buyer." I glance at her and wink, and a slight blush coats her cheeks.

"Coop!" she scolds me. "You're too much."

"If you're there, that's where I'm going to be," I tell her as I pull into my parents' driveway. "You gonna come in and say hi?" I ask, taking off my seat belt.

"Like your mom would let me get away with not," she says, staring out the windshield.

"If at any time you feel uneasy, let me know, and I'll take care of it. If I can't, I'll get us out of here."

"They're our parents, Cooper. We can't just leave."

"We can. You're my main priority. I've told my mom, and I know you've told yours. I don't think we have to worry about our fathers."

"Yeah, I can't see them saying much, if anything about this." She waves her hand between us.

"I don't either. Our mothers, on the other hand, I'm sure won't be able to keep quiet. Say the word, and we bail."

"Word." I reach for my seat belt and strap back in, making her laugh. "I was kidding."

"It's going to be fine." I don't think she's nervous about seeing them as much as she's nervous that they know we're… whatever it is we are right now. In my eyes, we're together. Reese still isn't putting a label on it, but we're exclusive, and our families know that.

"They're going to ask us what's going on."

"And I'll tell them that I'm madly in love with you and that as best friends, we're learning each other in a new capacity, and that it's our business. We'll include them when it's time."

"Wow, that sounds practiced."

"I knew this was going to be a concern for you."

"She's looking out the window," she says, nodding toward my parents' place.

"So is yours." I give the same nod to her parents' place.

"Come on then. Let's get this over with." She reaches for her handle, and before I can stop her to tell her I'll get the door, she's out of the car. It's probably for the best. That would just fuel our mothers on even more.

I follow her up the steps, and she stops at the door. "Go on in, babe. You never had to knock before," I say, placing my hand on the small of her back.

"It's different now."

"No, it's not different. It's better. This time when you walk into this house, it's not as my best friend, but as the love of my life. My future. Now, more than any time before, you belong here and don't need to knock. You're family. My family," I tell her. She smiles up at me, and that's how my mother finds us when she opens the door.

"Oh, look at you two. I missed you kids something awful," she says, pulling first Reese and then me into a hug.

"Mom, it hasn't even been two months since we saw you last."

"That's too long. Come on in. Dad's in the living room."

Dutifully, we follow her inside. Dad is in his recliner. "Welcome home." He smiles, turning off the television.

"Sit, sit." Mom points to the loveseat. We sit next to one another, and a glance at my mother tells me she's still beaming. "How are you? What's been going on?"

"Good. I've been enjoying some time off," I tell her.

"Reese, how's work?"

"Really good." She nods. "Stressful at times, but it's good."

"We're so proud of the two of you." Mom smiles.

Reading between the lines, she's also proud that we're together. She's not going to say it, but that's exactly what she's thinking. "What about the two of you? How are things?" I ask, leaning back into the loveseat.

Bliss | 103

"Oh, you know, same old. Snotty noses and potty breaks." Mom laughs. "The life of a kindergarten teacher."

"Dad? How's work?" He's a factory worker, been there since the week he graduated from high school.

"Doing well. We got a new line in at work, so I've been working some extra hours while we all get trained. Hey, while you're here, I got something I need some help with. You got a minute?" he asks.

"Sure." He stands, so I glance over at Reese. "You good, babe?" I ask, keeping my voice low, but I know my mother. Her hearing is impeccable, so I know she heard me.

"Of course." She smiles, but it's tight.

I can tell she's nervous. I want to lean in and kiss the stress right out of her, but pissing her off is not on the top of my list of things to do today. Instead, I wink and stand to follow Dad out to the garage.

"All right, old man, put me to work." I clap my hands and rub them together.

"I didn't really need any help," my dad confesses.

"Then why in the hell are we hanging out in the garage?" I was kidding when I called him an old man. He still has plenty of good years left, but now I'm starting to wonder. "You going senile on me?" I joke, only half kidding.

"Because I want to know how things are going?"

"Good. It's the off-season, so I'm just hanging out."

"Not that." He waves his hand in the air. "With Reese. How are things with Reese?"

"Did Mom put you up to this?" I question.

"No. Why would you think that? Never mind. So, how's it going?"

"Since when do you gossip?" I ask.

"Since my son started dating my best friend's daughter. A girl I've thought of as my own for over half of her life. Now, start talking," he says, looking behind him to make sure the door is still shut.

I chuckle. "Things are good, Dad."

"Good? That's all you've got for me?"

"I don't know what you want me to say. I love her. She's worried my feelings come from the fear of losing my best friend. We're taking our time, taking things slow."

"What does that mean? You kids these days. I don't understand the lingo."

"It means that I love Reese. That she is my person, and I'm giving her the time she needs. She loves me, I know she does, but she needs some time, and I'm giving her that. There's nothing else you need to know right now. When there is anything new or kind of development, I'll be sure to let you know."

"Are you going to ask her to marry you?"

"Yes. When the time is right."

"How do you know it's not right now?" he counters.

"Dad," I groan, rolling my eyes. "I know her. Trust me on this. She's not ready. We're not ready. She needs to understand, see, and feel my love for her. This is between the two of us. End of discussion."

"Cooper—" he starts, and I raise my hand to stop him.

"No. The end. Now, is there anything that I can help you with?"

"No," he grumbles good-naturedly.

"Good. Now let's get back inside to the women. Reese and I still need to go and say hi to her parents."

"Are you all staying here or there?" he asks.

"I'm staying here. She's staying there." I don't like it, but it is what it is.

"Son, I know—" he starts again, causing me to laugh.

"Dad. I'm staying at her place. In the spare room. Slow. That's how this is going."

"Oh, right. Slow," he agrees.

"Come on." I pat him on the shoulder and head back to the living room to find Mom and Reese right where we left them. "You ready to go say hi to your parents?" I ask her.

"Yes." She gives both my mom and dad a hug, and we walk through my parents' yard over to hers. "Mom, Dad, we're home!" she calls out.

I don't miss the "we're" part.

"Hey, kids," Eve greets us. "How was the drive?" she asks, giving Reese, then me, a hug, just as my mom did.

"Not bad. Coop did all the driving."

"It's like an hour and a half," I remind them.

"There's my girl," Garrett says, joining us in the kitchen.

I don't correct him and tell him she's mine. I'm thinking that won't go over all too well. Besides, he is her father, her first love. I can live with that. I smile to myself. I sound like a crazed lunatic, but that's how I am when it comes to Reese. I'm not fighting it anymore.

"Are you all hungry?" Eve asks.

"No, we stopped on the way," Reese tells her.

"Well, there's plenty when you're ready. I have to run to the store to pick up a few things. Do you want to ride with me?" Eve asks Reese.

She looks over at me, and I nod. "I'll head back over to Mom and Dad's," I say.

"Actually, Cooper, if you could stay a minute, I need help with something," Garrett asks.

"Sure." Leaning down, I kiss Reese on the top of her head. "Call me when you get back." I then give Garrett my full attention. "I'm all yours," I tell him.

"Out in the garage." He waves for me to follow him, and I do. "So, you two are living together," he says as soon as the door is shut to the house.

"Yes and no. I'm staying at her place in the spare room." He raises his eyebrows. "Trust me, I'm not happy about it either," I admit, and quickly curse under my breath. I forgot who I was talking to. *Son of a bitch.*

I wait for the backlash of my comment, but it never comes. Instead, a deep chuckle greets me. "That's more like it," he says with a smile.

"I'm confused."

"This 'we're taking it slow' business. I've heard it, Eve's heard it, your parents have heard it, and none of us are buying what the two of you are selling." He laughs.

"Well, I'm sorry to disappoint you. We are taking it slow. I'm sleeping in the spare room, but she's mine. She knows that. We're just not rushing into anything."

"She's her own woman, Cooper."

"I get that. I would never hold her back, but she's also the love of my life. That makes her mine. Yes, I'm aware she's not a possession, but she owns my heart." I shrug.

"There, you should have started with that."

"Is there something in the water? You and my dad both have cornered me, and we haven't been back an hour."

"Usually we get the gossip from our wives, but they're slacking in that department lately. Glad to see Trevor agrees with me, and it was time to just find out for ourselves."

"Is there anything else that you want to know?" I ask.

"No. I know you, Cooper. I know you're a man of your word, and I know you love my daughter. I've seen it for years. I'm just glad you finally pulled your head out of your ass." He grins.

"You and me both, Garrett. You and me both."

REESE

Mom ended up calling Ann and asking her if she wanted to ride with us. I assumed that meant they were both going to grill me about what's going on between Cooper and me. I was shocked, though, when neither one of them mentioned him, or our current situation. They talked my head off about the party they're having tomorrow night, and that they're glad Cooper and I could make it, but that was it.

The fact they didn't mention it made me want to. Sounds crazy, right? It's not even that I want to talk about him or us, because I don't. I know how I feel about it. I know that even with the best of intentions, and wonder woman efforts, I wasn't able to keep my heart from latching on to hope. The thing is, he's still holding strong on his declaration that he's in love with me. He's touching me and kissing me, and in front of our parents, and that's not who we are. Well, that's not who we were. This is altogether different, and I don't hate it.

Not even a little.

"So, I know that you don't want to talk about it," Mom says as we pull into the driveway. She glances at the passenger seat at Ann. "We both made up your rooms. We know you and Cooper are adults, and we don't care where you sleep, our place or theirs. We're just glad the two of you are home, and well, we're glad you're together."

"Th-anks," I say slowly. "Cooper will be staying with Ann and Trevor, and I'll be staying with you and Dad. He sleeps in the spare room at my apartment," I say again, even though I know they don't believe me.

"Oh," they both say at the same time. I'm in the back seat, but I can picture both of them with their mouths forming the perfect Os. These two have been best friends just as long as Cooper and me. In fact, so have our dads. Our families just hit it off, and the rest, as they say, is history. Well, it was until Cooper and I decided to complicate things. However, I must admit, our parents seem to be on board. I make a mental note to tell Cooper about this conversation.

Mom and I help Ann carry her items to her place and then unload ours. "How many people are coming to this party, anyway?" I ask.

"Well, we combined it again this year, so between the two houses, probably a hundred or so," Mom says nonchalantly.

"Do you know that many people?" I ask.

She laughs. "Yes, and that's combined. Your dad and Trevor are manning the grill over at their place, and Ann and I are doing the sides and desserts here. We plan to meet in the middle in the tent between the yards so everyone can gather together."

"Sounds like a lot of work."

"Parties usually are, but it's fun to catch up with people. Life seems to keep too busy during the year. Besides, you and Cooper are home for the first time since you left college for Memorial Day. We've stepped up our game, as you kids would say, since you've been gone. I'm sure everyone will be glad to see the two of you."

"Mom," I groan. "Please tell me that you didn't tell everyone we were dating. We don't even really have a name for what we are right now. We don't need all that added pressure."

"No. I didn't tell anyone, but, honey, one look at the way the two of you look at each other, and everyone is going to figure it out."

"Good to know. I should avoid Coop as much as possible tomorrow."

This time her laughter is loud and boisterous as she throws her head back. "Like that boy is going to let you avoid him."

"He's not a boy," I say, feeling my face heat. I know all too well that Cooper is all man.

"That—" She points at me with a huge grin on her face. "That look right there is going to give both of you away." Her comment is smug, and I don't reply because I have a feeling she might be right.

"You sure you want to do this?" I ask Cooper as we pull into Bill's Billiards.

"Are you kidding? I had to get out of the house. I love my parents, but I'm used to being on my own."

"To be honest, that's the only thing that got me here. I feel the same way," I confess.

"Come on. Let's go have a drink and catch up with some old friends." He pulls the keys from the ignition, and begrudgingly, I climb out and meet him in front of his truck. With his hand on the small of my back, he leads me inside.

My eyes scan the room, and I spy a small table in the back. Perfect. We can people watch, and hopefully not be seen. It's not that I don't want to see my old friends. It's more that I know what my mom said is true, and there is no way I can hide what Cooper means to me. The more I think about it and worry, I wonder why I need to? We're adults. We can do as we wish, with whomever we wish. My shoulders relax as we reach the table and take a seat.

"What do you want to drink?"

"Surprise me."

He winks, gives my shoulder a squeeze, and heads off toward the bar. I watch him until he gets lost in the crowd, and then I fight the urge to pull out my phone and scroll through random apps and my emails. My theory is if I don't make eye contact, then they will not engage. I'm being ridiculous, and I know that, but it doesn't stop me from reaching for my phone just as someone slides into the seat across from me.

"Reese!" Janie Henderson, my best friend in high school, says, wearing a grin. "I didn't know you were in town."

She didn't know because we lost touch when Cooper and I left for college. I also still have a hard time with the fact that she and Cooper slept together. She was his first. It's irrational, but it should have been me. More than that, she knew how I felt about him, and she was my best friend. It's wrong and petty, but I'll never forgive her for that. I'm well aware that if it wasn't Janie, it would have been someone else, but for me, she was my best friend. That made Cooper off-limits.

"Janie," I greet her.

"Are you here alone?" she asks.

Before I have a chance to answer, Joey Patrick, who coincidentally was my first, takes the seat next to her. "Reese Latham." He grins. "Didn't know you were back in town."

"I'm not. Just for the weekend visiting my parents."

"You should have called," Janie says, faking a pout.

"I'm only here for the weekend. Lots of family time. You know how it is."

"What's a gorgeous girl like you sitting here all alone?" Joey asks.

He's changed a good bit since high school. The beard he was always trying to grow back then now covers his face. It's not a sexy beard. It's more 'I'm too lazy to shave so I leave it there' kind of beard. Looking at him now, I can't believe that eighteen-year-old me slept with him. What in the hell was I thinking?

He reaches out and places his hand over mine, where it rests on the table. "You look good, Reese. Real good." He winks, and it takes everything in me not to roll my eyes.

Joey's eyes widen, and Janie's do too, so I know Cooper is back. "We should have known Cooper wasn't far behind. The two of you have always been thick as thieves," Joey says.

"Cooper," Janie purrs. It takes everything in me not to kick her underneath the table.

Cooper takes the seat next to me, places my drink in front of me, and pulls my hand from the table, placing it on his thigh. His arm goes around me, and he takes a sip of his beer before he addresses them. "Long time no see," he says. His voice is tight, and I know he's not impressed with their presence. I smile inwardly at getting to say I told you so later.

"There he is," Joey boasts. "Good season, my man."

"Thanks," Cooper says, taking another drink of his beer.

"Reese, save me a dance." Joey points at me as he stands.

"That won't be happening," Cooper says coolly.

"So, what? Are the two of you together?" Janie asks as if she can't believe it.

Cooper looks over at me and smiles. "If you call Reese being the love of my life us being together, then yeah. We're together."

I should be mad at him, but it's not a lie. We are dating, just a little unconventionally. He lives in another state, and things just sort of progressed from that first night when I agreed he could stay with me. He's still there, and I'm not the least bit mad about it. In fact, I can't imagine my apartment without him now. We're still keeping it low key, or at least we were. No doubt these two will spread that little nugget of information to the entire town.

"Oh, so you told him that you pined for him all through high school?"

"She didn't have to," Cooper answers before I can. "I told her first."

I pick up my bottle of beer and tilt it back. I drain it before setting it back on the table. I give Cooper a look that screams "save me," which he understands. Without touching the rest of his beer, he stands and offers me his hand. "Ready, baby?"

"Yes." I take his offered hand and let him pull me to my feet and into his arms.

"We've had a long day. We're going to head home. It was good seeing you both," Cooper says, even though we both know it was anything but.

I feel his lips press against the top of my head, and together, with his arm around my waist, we make our way out of the bar. "Well, that was a bust."

"Oh, the night's not over. We're just going to have our own party." Instead of guiding me to his truck, we walk next door to the gas station, and he buys a twelve-pack of beer.

"Where is this party taking place?" I ask him once we're back in his truck.

"The backyard, yours or mine, doesn't matter to me as long as you're there."

"Where was this idea earlier?" I inquire, loving this new development of our evening.

"You were right, dear," he says, teasing.

"Wait." I grab my phone from my purse and pull up the camera. "Okay. Now, say that again."

He chuckles and leans over the console, kissing me softly. "You were right, babe."

He's been touching me more since our night in the kitchen, pushing the boundaries. It's definitely not a hardship to have his hands on me. "Well, you better put this thing in gear. We have a party to get to."

Reaching over the console, he rests his hand on my thigh as we head toward home. Much like him, I don't care if we end up in my parents' backyard or his. As long as I get to spend time with him, that's all that matters.

Fifteen minutes later, we're pulling into his parents' driveway. "Where we headed, beautiful? Left or right?" he asks, removing his keys from the ignition.

I glance between the two houses and see all the lights off in my parents,' where a soft glow still shines through the living room window of his. "Right," I answer, choosing my parents' place. "I'm going to run in and change," I say, looking down at my jeans. "Meet you out back?"

"Yeah, I'm going to do the same. I'll bring the beer." He grins, and we both climb out of the truck, heading our separate ways.

As quietly as I can, I enter the house. It's dark, but that's okay. I have this place memorized. I slowly make my way upstairs to my old room and change into a pair of sweats and toss a hoodie over my T-shirt. It still gets cool at night this time of year, and tonight is no exception. Making my way back downstairs, I grab a quilt from the hall closet and quietly open the patio door and slip outside.

"I thought maybe you changed your mind." Cooper's deep voice greets me.

"Not a chance. I did stop and grab a blanket though." I hold it up so he can see.

"I got the fire started."

"It's a gas fireplace, Coop." I chuckle softly.

"But there's fire," he counters. He takes a seat on one of the lounge chairs and pats his lap. "Come sit with me."

I hesitate for a fraction of a second before giving in and doing as he asks. At this point, I'm tired of fighting it. It's what we both want. I settle on his lap, and he drapes the blanket over both of us, wrapping his arms around me.

"This is so much better than Bill's," he says, his lips next to my ear.

"Yeah. You should have started with this plan."

"Noted," he says with a low chuckle.

"It's so nice out here. I forgot what it's like to have a backyard this peaceful."

"We had the house in college," he reminds me.

"Peaceful, Coop. There was always so much going on, it was hard to just sit and chill like this."

"So, when we look for our place, a big quiet backyard is a must. Got it."

"Our place?"

"Yeah, I mean eventually, we're going to need more space. My condo is just a stepping-stone."

"You live in Indianapolis," I remind him.

"About that. I was hoping that maybe you could move there with me?" We're both quiet for a few minutes, and he keeps going. "I could keep my condo and stay there during the season, and then come home to you when I can, but that's long-distance, and I just don't think that I could do that with you."

I don't say anything as I process what he's saying. He's planning our future together. Not as my best friend, but as the love of my life. Not once since the day he walked into that banquet hall has he wavered on his feelings for me, and what we are, or what he wants us to be.

"The only other option is for me to walk away." I tense at his words, and his arms tighten around me. "You weren't listening to a damn thing I said. I'm not walking away from you, baby. If you were listening, you would have heard me say I would walk away from football."

"What?" I sit up and turn to look at him. "Cooper, are you crazy? You've worked your entire life to be where you are. This is your dream.

To play in the professional league. You can't just walk away. Not without good reason, and by good reason, I mean an injury or your health."

"Or the love of my life." With one hand still around my waist, he places the other against my cheek. "I mean it, Reese. I would give it all up if it means I get to be with you every day. To come home to you at night, to lie next to you as we fall asleep."

"Cooper, do you hear what you're saying?"

"I hear it, and I feel it. If that's what you want, for me to stay with you in Columbus, I'll do it. I spent a year of my life without you, and I never want to do that again. Never. If it takes walking away from football to achieve that, then so be it."

"You can't just walk away."

"Then come with me." Gently, he pulls my face to his. "I want it all, Reese. Every single moment life gives us, I want to spend it with you. I don't care what that looks like, or where we live, as long as we're together. You are what's important to me," he says before softly pressing his lips to mine.

I allow myself to get lost in the kiss. In the feeling of being wrapped up in his arms, knowing he wants me. Just me. It's a feeling of bliss I want to chase, and it's getting harder and harder not to. We spend hours, if I had to guess, in that chair, kissing and touching one another. Nothing overly sexual, but something you might do when you first start dating someone. When the dew and the chill of the night air set in, I know we need to head inside. Cooper pulls back from the longest kissing session in history and rests his forehead against mine.

"You should get inside."

"Yeah," I agree. Reluctantly, I untangle my body from his and the blanket and stand. He does the same, and we both stretch before Cooper turns off the fire pit.

He wraps his arms around me in a hug, burying his face in my neck. "Sweet dreams, beautiful. I'll see you in the morning." He pulls back and takes a hesitant step back.

"Coop." I hold my hand out for him.

"Yeah?" he asks, placing his hand in mine.

"Come with me." I begin to walk toward the house, the blanket in one hand, and Cooper's warm hand in the other. Quietly, we step inside, and he follows me upstairs to my room. I drop the blanket on the floor, pull off my hoodie, and climb into bed. Cooper just stands there in the moonlight, waiting for me to tell him what I want.

"Will you hold me?" I whisper into the dark quiet of the room.

I hear him exhale. "Nothing I want more," he murmurs. The bed dips and I'm in his arms, snuggled under the blankets.

I don't think about what it means or how our parents are going to react when they find out we stayed together. No, the only thing I'm thinking about is how tonight has been one of the best I've ever had. Just me and Cooper. Together. Not hanging with my best friend, but a man who loves me. With each passing day, with each tender caress, my heart begins to heal, and the love I have for him grows.

More than that, I begin to believe he's really in this for me. For us.

Chapter 15

COOPER

"School has only been out for two weeks, and already the kids are going stir crazy. I just wish there was funding to take them somewhere, like the zoo or COSI or something. Things are tight at the state level, and honestly, they just worry about keeping the kids fed, clothed, and a roof over their heads. I guess I just feel like I know what they are missing out on, you know?"

"Is there anything we can do?"

"Fundraising is difficult, and many forget we even have a children's home. It makes me realize how fortunate we were growing up. I mean, some of these kids come to the home with their meager belongings in trash bags, some worse off come with nothing. It's heartbreaking."

"Come here." I pull her closer to me and kiss the top of her head. Since that weekend at her parents,' I've been sleeping in her bed every night. We're still taking it slow, so no sex. But there has been a lot of kissing and touching. My hands have memorized every dip and every curve of her body.

"I'm sorry. I know you're probably tired of hearing about all of this."

"No. I want to be the person you can turn to. I don't care what you have to say. I'm going to listen."

She rolls over to face me. "I love having you here. Not just here in my bed, but in my apartment and in my life."

I don't hide my grin. She's still kept her feelings tight to her chest. I'm still waiting for those three little words, but I'm not worried. I know they'll come. "There is nowhere else I'd rather be." I kiss the top of her head. "Speaking of, I need to go to Indy next week. I have to meet with my agent to sign a couple of endorsement deals. Do you think you could get off work on Friday? We could spend the weekend at my condo. If not, we can just leave when you get off work."

"You don't have to wait on me, and I don't have to go with you."

"Yes, I do. Yes, you do. I have training camp in a little over a month, and I'm going to be leaving. That means I need all the time with you that I can get."

"Are you excited for the season?"

"Yeah, I think we're going to go far this year."

"Of course you will," she says, quick to support my team and me.

"You going to be at some of my games?"

"I'll try."

I want to tell her to quit the damn job and come with me. She could come to all the games, but I don't. I have plans in the making, and I need to time it all just right. I haven't brought up me leaving football again, but I would for her, and I wouldn't think twice about it. No regrets.

"Well, I'm just going to throw this out there so that there is no confusion. I want you there. I want you at as many games as possible. I'll fly you there, and I'll have a seat for you at every stadium."

"Okay." One word, but I can tell by the tone of her voice that she's pleased. "I should get some sleep."

"I love you." I kiss the top of her head again. She doesn't reply, but she snuggles into my chest. I feel her love. She doesn't have to say it, although I'm dying to hear those three little words from her, I feel them every single day. That's enough for now. We've come a long way in just a couple of months.

"Have a good day, baby." I press my lips to the corner of her mouth and open the door for her. I need to give her some time to get to work to know the coast is clear, so I grab a quick shower before setting my plans in motion. I can't call until eight anyway.

After a quick internet search, I have a name and number to call, so I dial the phone and wait. "Mr. Garcia, this is Cooper Reeves." After answering questions about the Defenders, and promising an autograph, I get to the reason for my call.

"Mr. Reeves, that's very generous of you. If you don't mind me asking, what prompted all of this?"

"Reese Latham is my girlfriend. She expressed how the kids don't get to go out and do much, and I'd like to help."

"Certainly," he agrees, just as he did a few minutes ago when I laid out my plan.

"I'd like to make this happen as soon as possible."

"Well, we have plenty of workers at the home. We should be able to arrange this whenever you want."

"Today. I also would like for Reese to be able to attend with us."

"That's not an unfair request. She is their social worker. We'll have to take two vans," he comments.

"No. I'll take care of that too. If you could let the workers know, and the kids. Just keep my name out of it. I'll be there at noon to pick them all up. I'll have transportation."

"Sure. Thank you, Mr. Reeves. This is going to mean a lot to those kids. Oh, and your agent sent over all of the background checks. Thank you for that. It's important we know that the children are safe."

"Don't thank me. Thank Reese. She's the one who cares enough to talk about those kids at home each night. I never would have thought to do this without her. As far as the background checks, as a team we do a lot of charity work, so all the players have routine background checks. We'll talk soon," I say, ending the call. I have transportation to arrange.

Three hours later, I pull up to the children's home and see the bus that I ordered waiting. Locking up my truck, I walk to the door to talk to the driver. "Hi, I'm Cooper." I shake his hand. "Thank you for being here on such short notice," I tell him.

"It's not every day the boss calls you on your day off for a special request from a professional athlete," he jokes. "Sam Landerson, nice to meet you." He offers me his hand.

Sam is an older gentleman, probably in his early sixties, if I had to guess. "I brought my wife." He points to the first seat on the bus. "I hope that's okay. We don't get to see our own grandkids as often as we'd like, and this sounded like a good day to us."

"That's more than okay. I'm glad you're both here. I'm going to run in and get the kids, and we'll be ready to go."

"We'll be waiting," he assures me.

With a smile and a wave, I exit the bus and make my way to the front door. "Hi, I'm here to see Todd Markum," I tell the receptionist.

"Oh." Her eyes light up. "Yes, he's expecting you. I'll buzz you through." She hits the button and the lock on the door releases. "Right this way." She motions for me to follow her.

"Cooper!" Todd Markum stands and greets me. "It's a pleasure to meet you."

"Likewise," I say, shaking his hand. "Are we all set?"

"Yes, but I didn't tell the kids or the staff. Just told them to prepare for an outing. They're all waiting in the common room. I thought I'd let you tell them."

"Great. Lead the way." I follow him out of his office and down a long hallway that I know ends in the common room for the kids.

"Kids," he says, and all heads turn our way.

"Coop?" Reese asks in confusion when she spots me.

"Hey." I go to her and wrap her in a hug. I want to do more, but I know she's working.

"What are you doing here?"

"Well," I say, looking away from her to the kids. "I thought we could take a trip."

"What kind of trip?" Hank, the youngest of the group, asks.

"We're going to the zoo."

"Really?" the oldest, Jeff asks.

"Yep."

"When?" Reese asks.

"Now. Are you guys ready to go?"

"Cooper?" Reese asks.

"Ms. Latham. It's all been arranged. Mr. Reeves has funded the outing, and there's plenty of staff to go and keep an eye on the kids. You will be going as well."

I feel her gaze, so I look down to find her peering up at me with tears in her eyes. "You…." She shakes her head, biting down on her bottom lip.

I lean in close and whisper, "I love you," then stand to my full height. "Now, before we go, I need your word that you'll be on your best behavior. Can you do that?" I ask the twelve sets of wide, innocent eyes that stare back at me. Head nods, and a chorus of "Yes!" echoes throughout the room. "Great. Now, there's a bus parked right outside. Everyone go load up. Ms. Reese and I will be there in just a minute."

There is a flurry of activity while the workers and the kids head outside to the bus. "Thank you." I hold my hand out for Todd. "For allowing me to do this for them."

"Thank you for wanting to. This is a rare treat for them. We appreciate what you're doing."

"Like I said, thank Reese. Without her, this wouldn't have happened." He nods and turns to leave.

"Cooper," Reese says once it's just the two of us. "I can't believe you did this."

"You said the kids didn't get to go out, and there was no funding, so I made it happen."

"I can't believe this. You are an amazing man, Cooper Reeves." Her smile lights up her face.

"Behind every good man is a great woman." I kiss the corner of her mouth. Sure, it's cliché as fuck, but it makes her smile grow wider so it's worth it. Besides, it's the truth. I wouldn't be the man I am today without her. She's helped shape my past, and I can't wait to see the way our future together unfolds. "Now, let's get moving. There is fun to be had." Placing my hand on the small of her back, I lead her outside to the bus.

"A party bus?" She laughs.

"Hey, it was short notice, and I promise you the kids will like the lights and the music. I wanted everyone to be able to ride together. This

Bliss | 123

should be a bonding experience for them. They don't get this often, and I want it to be a happy memory for them. My hope is that this bright day can outshine some of the dark ones."

She's smiling up at me, but her eyes are shimmering with tears. "I know the kids are watching us, eager to see where today is going to take us, but I want to kiss you so bad right now."

"Then do it." My voice is husky, even to my own ears.

"Later. When we get home."

"Promise?"

She nods. "I promise."

"Get your fine ass on that bus. We've got some fun to get to." She laughs but moves to climb on the bus, and I follow her. "All right, you ready for a fun day?" I ask the kids.

"Yeah!" they cheer.

"Remember, you have to listen to what we tell you. No running off. You have to stay with us at all times. Got it."

"Got it," they all eagerly agree.

"Sam, to the zoo!" I throw my arm in the air, and the kids cheer. I take a seat next to Reese and just sit back and listen to their excited chatter. If feels good to know I could do this for them. Their smiles are contagious, as are those of my girl when she looks over at me. "Thank you," she mouths.

"I love you," I mouth back.

Her smile grows, as does my heart in my chest.

"Look at them," Reese says, leaning into me. We're on our way home from the zoo. We closed it down. Stayed until they kicked us out, and the kids, even though sleeping, are still wearing smiles while clutching onto their prizes. "You spoiled them today, Coop. I don't know how I will ever thank you for this."

"I don't need your thanks, Reese. I did it because I wanted to. Besides, it was you who told me they didn't get this kind of thing. I never would have thought of it had it not been for you."

"This must have cost you a fortune."

"You remember I signed my new contract last week, right?" I ask her.

"Yeah, but, Cooper, this was a lot of money."

"Reese, I can afford it."

"I know. At least I think I do, but this was a lot."

"Baby, my contract was for fifteen million."

"Yes, but that has to last you. And there's taxes and living expenses and—" I place my hand over her mouth.

"Fifteen million a year for five years." Her eyes widen. "How did you not know that?"

"I don't know. You never mentioned the amount, just that it was a sweet deal, and I went with it. It wasn't my place to ask."

"If it involves me, it is your place. Make it your business, Reese. Me... make *me* your business."

"That's... a lot of money."

"It is. We're going to invest and spend wisely, and we should be set for life. Especially when you add in my endorsement deals."

"He's kind of a big deal, Ms. Reese," a groggy Jeff tells Reese.

"You." She chuckles softly. "I thought you were sleeping."

"Just resting my eyes."

"Come here, you." She pulls him into a hug, and I can visibly see him relax into her hold.

These kids are starved for love and affection, and my girl, she's giving it to them in spades. I'm so damn proud of her, and I cannot only see but empathize with her frustration with the system. There is so much more she could be doing. So many more kids she could be helping.

When we make it back to the home, Reese and the other staff help guide the kids inside. I stay back with Sam and Dorothy. "I can't thank you both enough for today. I know it was last minute and it was a long one, but it's a day those kids will never forget."

"Son, we were happy to be a part of it. It's a good thing you did." Sam nods.

"Thank you. This is for you." I reach into my pocket and pull out the two-hundred-dollar tip I set aside for them.

"That's not necessary. We had just as much fun as they did," Sam tells me.

"It's true. That little one, boy, oh boy, he reminds me of our grandson. Today was good for the soul," Dorothy adds.

"Please, I insist. I could not have pulled this off without your services. Thank you."

Sam shakes his head, so I reach out and slide the bills into his shirt pocket. "Be safe driving home," I tell them, stepping off the bus. I'm halfway to the door when Reese steps out. Her purse and laptop bag slung over her shoulder.

"I'll drive," I tell her.

"I have to be back in the morning."

"I know. I'll drive you. Come on." I hold my hand out for her and she takes it with ease.

The drive home is quiet. I have so many things on my mind, plans I'm making, wishes I'm wishing, that I'm lost in my head. When we pull into the parking lot of her building, and I turn off the truck, I glance over to see her watching me.

"What you did today, Coop, I know it was meant to be for the kids, but it meant so much to me. The fact that you listen to me when I talk, that you took action to make a memory for those twelve boys that they will never forget…. It's a day *I* will never forget."

"I didn't do it just for them. I did it for you too. I know them being cooped up weighs heavy on your mind. I know you were worried about them not getting to experience life. It was something small I could do for you and for them."

"It was perfect," she says, covering a yawn.

"Come on. Let's get you to bed," I say as she reaches for her handle to climb out of my truck.

"I need a shower." She yawns again as we enter her apartment.

"Me too." Is it too much to hope she'll ask me to join her?

"I'll make it quick," she says, moving down the hall.

I guess I got my answer. Making sure the door is locked, I go to my room, the one I no longer sleep in and strip down to my underwear, grabbing a clean pair to sleep in. Walking across the hall, I plug my phone in to charge and then head back to the living room to grab hers and do the same thing. All while, I'm trying to ignore the fact she's naked and wet just behind the bathroom door. I stand outside the door, tempted to join her, but think better of it. The water shuts off, and I high tail it back to her room, so I'm not busted creeping outside the bathroom door.

"All yours," she announces.

I look up to find her hair up in a towel, and another wrapped around her body. All that separates me from her is one piece of thick cotton. My cock begins to harden just thinking about seeing her like that again.

"Coop," she says, waving her hand in my face. I blink and look up at her. She's now standing in front of me. "You okay?"

"No," I manage to croak out. I see the worry on her face, so I grab her hand and place it over my now rock-hard erection. "This is what you do to me."

"Oh." Her eyes widen, but I see heat there.

"Oh, is right. I'm going to shower. Please be dressed when I get back."

"Or what?"

"Or I might have to sleep in my room in order to keep my hands off you." She nods, but I can see what my words do to her. Her chest is rising and falling as if it's hard for her to take a breath, and her tongue peeks out to lick her lips. I stand and step around her. "I love you, baby, but you're too fucking tempting," I say as I rush down the hall to take a cold shower.

Chapter 16

REESE

"Are we there yet?" I tease Cooper.

"No." He squeezes my thigh, where his hand has been resting the majority of this trip. "We're going to meet with my agent at the stadium to sign the contracts, and then we'll head to my condo."

"Are you excited about your deals?"

"As excited as a man can be to have pictures taken of him in his underwear." He laughs.

"Should I be jealous? The women of the world are going to be ogling you."

"No. There is nothing for you to be jealous about. Besides, you're the only one who gets to see what's underneath."

"I don't know. Have you seen some of those underwear commercials?" I ask him.

"Yes, and trust me, there is nothing to worry about."

"So, what else is on the agenda for this weekend?"

"Nothing really. I just want to spend time with you. I thought I could show you around the city a little bit. You'll get to see the stadium today."

"Do you like it here?"

He shrugs, keeping his eyes on the road. "Honestly, I'm not really sure. Last year was hard for me. I didn't really let myself take it all in."

"What do you mean?"

"I missed you, Reese. It was hard, and I spent a lot of my time brooding because of it. I got close to a couple of guys on the team, but for the most part, I stayed to myself. I didn't go out with them, unless it was at one of their houses. I just… wasn't feeling any of it without you being there with me."

"I guess we need to talk about that, huh? You'll be coming back soon." How can my heart be soaring with his confession and falling to the pit of my stomach in a matter of seconds? I know he has to leave. It's his job, I've always known our situation isn't permanent, but that doesn't make the pain of knowing I'm not going to see him every day lessen. Then there's him telling me how hard it was for him. I wasn't alone in my struggle. If I would have spent less time avoiding him, and more time speaking my mind, a lot of pain, ours and Hunter's, could have been avoided.

"Yeah," he agrees. "I don't want to talk about that right now. I want to enjoy you being here with me."

"Okay, but we need to talk about it." I'm not ready for him to go back, but I know it's his job and would never in a million years ask him to give that up. He's worked so hard to get where he is. I just don't know how we are going to manage with long distance.

I've been looking online for social worker positions in the area, and so far, I've not had much luck. I enjoy what I do, and I would miss the kids I'm working with, but if it meant being with Cooper all the time, I would move. He's mentioned it, but we've not talked about it. We also haven't talked about us, and I know that's all on me. I've been keeping us in the safe zone, but the reality is there is no safe zone. Not when it comes to Cooper. I'm madly in love with him. That is the one thing I'm certain of. I know that no matter the time or the distance, he still owns my heart. I was never willing to admit that until now.

"Ready?" he asks, pulling me out of my thoughts.

"Yes." I give him a wide smile. "I'm excited to see your new stomping grounds."

"Business first." He pulls the keys from the ignition and reaches for the handle.

I do the same and meet him at the front of his truck. "Oh my God! Are you Cooper Reeves, I love you so much! I'm your biggest fan," I say, sugary sweet and jumping up and down.

He throws his head back and laughs, snaking his arm around my waist. "My biggest fan, huh?"

"Oh, the biggest," I say, giggling.

"And you love me?" he asks with a glint of humor in his eyes.

"I want to have your babies."

He pulls me into his chest and wraps his arms around me. "You love me, and you want to have my babies. Sold." He pulls back, and we begin to walk toward the building. "How did you know that's all I've ever wanted?"

"What's that?" I ask, confused.

"You to love me and have my babies." He smirks and pulls open the doors.

My steps falter but quickly recover as his agent, Jarvis Jones, comes walking toward us. "Right on time," he says, leaning in to kiss my cheek. "Reese, good to see you."

"You too." I'm surprised he remembered my name. I only met him a couple of times, and that was over a year ago.

"Cooper, you ready? This won't take long. I've had legal comb through both contracts, and it's good to go."

"Both?" I ask.

"Oh, in addition to underwear, there's a sports drink that picked me up too," Cooper explains.

"Your boy's going to be a household name," Jarvis tells me.

Cooper smiles at me, and if I'm not mistaken, there is a slight blush to his cheeks. I'd call him out on it, but I don't want to make it worse in front of his agent. He's supposed to be this bigtime badass football player. He is that, but he's also just Cooper.

"Come on into the conference room. I have it all squared away," Jarvis says, motioning for us to follow him.

Bliss | 131

"Mary." Cooper stops as a lady about our parents' age passes us in the hall. "Thank you so much for sending me all of the gear. This is my girlfriend, Reese. She works as a social worker for the children's home, where I took the items," he explains.

"Nice to meet you, Reese." She offers me her hand, which I shake. "I hate to run, but I have a meeting across town." She waves and rushes down the hall.

Cooper starts to walk again, and I have to rush to catch up with him, not that he's giving me a choice. He hasn't let go of my hand. We follow Jarvis into the conference room, and I sit and watch as Cooper signs two contracts for endorsement deals. It's surreal to watch. I love that I get to be here for this moment. He's made it. He did it, and I'm so damn proud of him. This is more than just a stadium. This is his work, his blood, sweat, and tears, and I get to be here with him.

We talked about this day so many times, him going pro. It's here, he's living it, and although he's headed into his second season, it's really sinking in for me being here. I tried so much to not think about him all last year, I missed out on all of this. The excitement, and the thrill of him living his dream.

"That's it," Jarvis says, placing the signed contracts into a folder. "I'll send these over, and I'll be in touch about the next steps."

"Thanks, Jarvis."

"That's my job. What are you two getting into the rest of the day?" he asks, making conversation.

"I thought about giving Reese a tour."

"They're painting, so that won't be today. Next weekend?"

"Yeah, maybe," Cooper says, not committing. He looks over at me. "I guess we're heading home. It's been a while. I'm sure the place needs airing out."

"Call me if you need anything," Jarvis says, leaving the room with some pep in his step. Not that I blame him. Cooper signing those two deals, in addition to his new five-year contract, Jarvis just got another big payday.

"Home sweet home," Cooper says, unlocking his condo, and pushing the door open, motioning for me to walk in first. "It smells better than the last time I was here."

"Bad?" I ask, smiling.

"You have no idea. I cleaned out the fridge and washed up the laundry when I came down that day and signed my new contract."

"Coop, it's a great space, but it barely looks lived in," I say, looking around the room. There are no pictures on the walls or any other types of decorations that make this place his.

"I slept here. Hung out on the couch watching TV, that's about it." He points to the end table.

I walk toward the end table and look down at the one and only decoration. A framed picture of the two of us. Picking it up, it's a picture of us that was taken at one of his CU games. He's in his jersey and a sweaty mess, but we're both smiling and happy.

"I love that one," Cooper says.

"I've never seen it."

"Mom took it. Junior year."

I set the frame back on the table as my eyes scan the room. My eyes seek out something that I might have missed, but come up empty. Just me and him. The realization of that sucks the air from my lungs. It's not that I didn't believe him that last year was hard for him. I guess I just never let myself believe it was as bad as he said it was.

"Tour?" he asks, holding his hand out for me, and I take it, letting him pull me from the couch. "This is the living room." He grins and leads me toward the kitchen. "Eat-in kitchen. There's a decent-sized patio out back with a grill and a couple of lawn chairs. I don't do much entertaining.

"I have two bedrooms and two full bathrooms. My room has a master bath, then the guest bath, which whoever is in the second bedroom also has to use," he explains, leading me down the hall. "Guest bath." He points out.

"Have a lot of overnight guests, do you?" I ask him before I can think better of it.

"No. None actually, you're the first." He leads me to the end of the hallway. There is a small closet door directly in front of us and a door on both sides of the wall. "Right side master, left side guest room. Go

Bliss | 133

ahead and look around. I'm going to run out to the truck and grab our bags." He kisses my temple and leaves me standing in the hall.

Curiosity gets the best of me as I step into his room. The same comforter he used at college is sprawled across his bed. There's a dresser, and an empty clothes basket on the far wall, and a nightstand on either side of the bed. There are no pictures or art on the walls. It's very manly, and very Cooper. It just feels like it's not really home. My eyes land on another frame, all by itself, on what must be his side of the bed. My feet carry me to that side of the bed as my eyes narrow in on the picture.

It's me. I don't recognize where I am, but I'm smiling and looking off in the distance. I pick it up to get a closer look, trying to pinpoint when and where this was taken.

"That one," Cooper says from behind me, "is my favorite."

"I don't recognize it." I don't look away from the picture.

"That's because I cropped me out of it." He walks over to me and pulls open the nightstand drawer, pulling out a single photograph, and hands it to me.

My hands tremble as I take it from him, and suddenly, I not only recognize the picture, but I'm taken back to that day. I can remember the smells, the sounds, and even the moment. In the original picture, my smile, it's for Cooper. He's looking at me, wearing the same grin. It was our high school graduation party. Our parents combined them, and Coop and I had just finished singing karaoke.

"I remember that day."

"Me too. Although, I admit now I see it differently. I see the way we looked at each other even back then, and I kick myself in the ass for not realizing what we were. I was too blind to see that you have always been more than my best friend, Reese. I'm sorry it took me so long."

Staring down at the picture, I see it. All the times we've had together, and more importantly, that look. It's the same one I've seen on him every day since he came busting into the room at the banquet hall, telling me he loves me.

This is us, and it's real. It's not something that's just going to go away. Our love, it's so much more than what I think either of us dreamed it could be. It's a "deep-rooted in your chest, chains around your heart" kind of love.

Carefully, I place the picture back into the nightstand and close the drawer. Then, I turn to face him. It takes me one step to be toe to toe with him. It takes one second for my hands to rest against his cheeks. It takes one heartbeat for me to say, "I love you, Cooper Reeves."

He leans down and presses his lips to mine. It starts out slow, his hands clasping behind my back, mine resting on his face, but then his hands begin to roam, and all bets are off. I take a step back, stepping out of his hold, grab the hem of my T-shirt, and pull it over my head. His brown eyes watch me intently as I go to the waistband of my capris and quickly remove them. I kick them off to the side.

"Jesus, Reese." Cooper reaches for me, but I take another step back, my legs hitting the bed.

"You're wearing too many clothes," I say as I reach behind me and unclasp my bra, slowly sliding the straps over my shoulders and letting the silky garment fall to the floor.

"Cooper," I say when he just stands there staring at me.

"This is real. Right? Please tell me I'm not dreaming." His eyes rake over my body.

"This is real," I assure him.

"Thank fuck," he mutters before quickly shedding his clothes. His hands grip my waist as he picks me up and sets me on the bed. "Lie back, baby."

I do as I'm told, anxious for his hands and his mouth and his cock, in any order. I've denied us both long enough. "Cooper," I pant as he kisses my ankle, moving his lips to trail up to my inner thigh. He kisses me over my panties, but all too quickly, his lips are gone and are on my opposite thigh, trailing kisses down my leg.

"Lift for me," he says once he's done torturing me. I lift my hips, and he slides my panties down my legs, dropping them to our collective pile on the floor.

"I don't have condoms here," he says, his voice tight. "I didn't think this would happen, or I would have been more prepared."

"We didn't use one last time. I'm still on the pill."

"I didn't want to assume."

"You're my boyfriend. We're in a committed, loving relationship. If we're both comfortable with it, we don't have to use them."

"Are you? Tell me what you want, Reese."

"I want you inside me. Sooner rather than later."

His eyes flare with heat. "Bare?" he asks, choking on the word.

"Only you," I remind him.

"Only you," he says in return.

Chapter 17

COOPER

I take a minute to just look at her. To stare at the beauty lying before me. I've wanted for this for what feels like an eternity, wanted us, and now that she's here, and all mine, I don't know where to start.

I want all of her. There are so many things I want to do to her, but there are two that I need before any of the others. First, I need to hear her tell me she loves me again. I've waited so long to hear those words, and I just… need her to say it again. Two, I need to taste her. Now. My mouth waters at the thought.

"Say it again," I demand, my voice husky with my desire for her.

"Only you."

"No, tell me," I say, leaning in and placing a kiss just below her belly button. I peer up at her as she lifts up on her elbows to look me in the eye.

"I love you, Cooper."

"Fuck, baby, you don't know what hearing you say that does to me." I slip my finger through her folds, and she moans. I lick my lips. She's so wet. The anticipation is killing me. I lean in close, ready to fucking devour her, when her words stop me.

"Coop."

I glance up to see her still sitting up on her elbows, her teeth biting at her bottom lip. "I don't know if—I mean, I've never." She nods toward where I'm on my knees between her legs, preparing to devour her.

"We're going to learn together. You tell me what you like, and if I do something you don't like, tell me that too." She nods, her teeth still chewing on that bottom lip. Lowering my mouth, I swirl my tongue over her clit, and she moans.

"Oh my God," she breathes.

Her reaction is all the confidence I need to keep going. I nip, and suck, and lick, all while she squirms beneath me. I love that I'm driving her crazy, that she yearns for my touch. Heavy and throbbing, my cock's reminding me I need to be inside her. To feel her pulse around me. I need her to come. Sliding one finger into her heat, I pump lazily a few times before sliding another, and sucking her clit into my mouth.

"Oh, fuck!" she cries.

Her pussy pulses around my fingers and her orgasm explodes on my tongue. I take all that she's giving me, not stopping until her body relaxes into the mattress. Then, and only then, do I slowly remove my fingers from her and wipe my mouth with the back of my arm.

Sitting back on my knees, I watch her closely as her chest rapidly rises and falls, and her eyes slowly open.

"Hi," she says shyly.

"I love you."

A slow lazy smile pulls at her lips. "I love you too."

Climbing to my feet, I grip my cock in my hand and pump a few times. Her eyes zone in on my actions. "Move back on the bed, Reese." She does as I ask, and again, I just take her in. Her hair is splayed out on the pillow, her eyes hooded and hungry, and her body is flushed from her release.

"You need help with that?" she asks.

"Just enjoying the view," I tell her.

"My view's not so bad either, but I was kind of hoping for the full experience."

"I'm a full-service kind of guy." I chuckle, climbing onto the bed and settling between her thighs. She immediately wraps her legs around my waist, locking them behind my back.

"Now I've got you." She laughs.

"I never want you to let me go."

She moves her head from side to side. "Never."

Bending my head, I kiss her. It's slow and deep as my tongue pushes past her lips. I push inside her. Home. Reese is and will forever be home to me. I push all the way in and pull out of the kiss, resting my forehead against hers.

"This is real, right? We're together. No holding back, no hiding. It's you and me. We can start planning our future?"

"It's real. *We're* real. I couldn't hold back any longer, even if I wanted to. It's killed me to keep you at arm's length all this time."

"You let me hold you at night," I say, kissing her cheek. "And hold your hand," I add, placing a kiss to the other cheek. "You let me live with you." I kiss her nose. "You let me love you," I whisper as my lips press to hers.

The time for talking is done as I make love to her. Over and over again, I slide in and out of her body, each time feeling as though I go deeper and deeper. Holding my weight on my arms on either side of her head, I stare down at her and get lost in her eyes, lost in her soul. It's not just our bodies that tether us, but our hearts. The connection is powerful and overwhelming. Our first time was fast and intense, years of pent-up sexual frustration with one another, causing us to go fast and hard. This time though, we take our time. Her hands stroke my arms, my back, before she rests them on either side of my face.

"I'm close, Coop."

"Thank fuck." I swivel my hips and thrust a little harder, a little faster, and that's all it takes for her nails to dig into my arms, her back to arch off the bed, and my name to fall from her lips as her pussy squeezes my cock like a vise.

I try to hold off, but the sensation is just too much. As my body stills, I release inside her. It's a feeling I can't explain. The magnitude of the trust we share, and the thought that one day she's going to be growing round with our baby. My cock twitches at the mere thought, causing us both to moan with pleasure.

My lips connect with hers before I slowly pull out and settle in beside her. I open my mouth to tell her that I love her when my phone rings. I let it ring, and Reese rolls over to look at me.

"It might be important."

"You're more important," I say, kissing the top of her head and pulling her close. My phone stops ringing only to start again.

"Coop, you better get that."

Reluctantly, I climb out of bed and dig around for my phone in my jeans pocket when I see it's my attorney. "Hey, John," I greet him.

"Cooper, how are you?" he asks.

"Never better," I say, glancing back at the love of my life snuggled naked under the covers in my bed.

"Glad to hear it. Listen, I have everything all set up. I just need signatures. When are you available?"

"How long are you in the office today?" I ask him, glancing at the alarm clock beside the bed.

"A few more hours at least."

"Reese and I are in town. I had some contract stuff to sign with my agent. We could be there in say an hour?"

"Perfect. It's good she's with you. We can get this all done today."

"Definitely. Thank you, John. We'll see you soon." I end the call and place my phone on the nightstand.

"See, I told you it might be important. Everything okay?" she asks.

"Yes. I actually have a surprise for you. It's ready sooner than I had anticipated. We need to get ready. I need to run a few errands while we're out."

"Where are we going?" she asks, sitting up and letting the blanket pool around her waist. I climb onto the bed and capture a nipple between my teeth, gently nipping before sucking it into my mouth. "Coop," she breathes.

"I can't fucking resist you," I tell her, letting her nipple fall from my lips and moving to the next one.

"I thought you said that we had to get ready to go somewhere."

Damn it. "Yeah," I say, releasing her and moving off the bed. "You go shower. I can't go in there with you or we're never leaving, and we have things to do."

"Where are we going?"

"To my attorney's office. I have some more papers to sign," I say vaguely.

"Okay. I'll be quick."

"He's just about ten minutes away, so you have time."

I watch her as she stands and goes to her bag and grabs some clean clothes. "Everything you need should be in the bathroom. Check the closet for towels, and your favorite shampoo and body wash should be there too."

"How? When?" She looks at me, surprised.

"I wanted to be prepared if you were to ever come stay with me." I shrug like it's not a big deal. To me, it isn't. I just wanted her to feel welcome here, and maybe even fall in love with not only me but this place. However, I see the shimmer of emotion in her eyes, and I know it's a bid deal to her. "Go." I wave toward the bathroom. "Or I'm going to have to call him and tell him we have to reschedule," I say, glancing down at my cock that's already starting to grow hard for her yet again.

"I'm going." She smiles and disappears behind the door.

Grabbing some clean clothes, I go to the bathroom down the hall and shower. I make a mental note that showering with Reese is absolutely the next item on our to-do list. After I give her this surprise. I'm not sure how she's going to take it. I hope it's received well.

"So, what kind of papers do you need to sign?" Reese asks as we're walking into the attorney's office.

I was lucky Tessa called and talked to her all the way here; otherwise, I would have had to think of something on the fly. What's luckier is that John greets us as soon as we walk through the door.

"Cooper, good to see you." He extends his hand, and we shake.

"You too. John, this is my girlfriend, Reese Latham. Reese, John, my attorney." They exchange handshakes and pleasantries before John leads us back to his office.

"I didn't expect to get both signatures today, but that will move this process along nicely," John says.

"Coop?" Reese whispers.

"Actually, John. Reese doesn't know why we're here. Would you mind going over the details for her?" I ask him. I know that if I try to do it, I'll fuck it up. Not only that, I want to be able to watch her reaction as she hears what I've done.

If John is shocked that I haven't told her yet, he doesn't show it. "Of course," he replies. He moves some papers around and then looks up at Reese. "Cooper has set forth the motion to create a nonprofit organization."

"Cooper." Reese turns her head to look at me. "That's amazing."

"There's more," I say, smiling at her.

"These papers are the official filing for the nonprofit status," John explains.

"What kind of nonprofit?" she inquires.

I nod at John. "The foundation will be set to help foster children. The conditions are clearly outlined. The foundation will provide suitcases and duffle bags for the children's personal belongings," he begins to explain. Reese keeps her eyes on his but reaches over and squeezes my hand. "Without giving you every detail, there will be things such as transition help for those going on to college, celebrations for those who are placed and adopted. Scholarships will be awarded each year, as well as group activities for those in children's homes. That's the basic idea of the foundation. I have a copy of the full outline with details of the foundation for each of you."

"I don't understand?" Reese says, glancing over at me.

"It's not just my foundation, baby. It's ours. We both have to sign today. I'll be the President, and my job is to silently fund it, and hopefully use my career for fundraising and awareness. You are listed as the executive director of the foundation. You run it all. It's all in your capable hands."

"What does that mean?" she asks with tears in her eyes.

"It means that all the things you wished that you could do for your kids, you can do. Only this is on a grander scale. You will have free rein to organize fundraising and distribution of supplies, and everything else that's involved. It's a startup, so there will be a lot of work to get it off the ground."

"I-I can't believe you did this."

"You said you wanted to do more. I'm giving you the power to do that."

"Cooper." She sobs my name as she covers her face with her hands.

"I'm going to step out and give the two of you a few minutes. Just open the door when you're ready," John says, standing and leaving us alone in his office.

"Come here." I pull her from her chair and place her in my lap. My arms wrap around her as I hold her close. Her tears come fast, but I'm there to catch them. "I thought this would make you happy," I say, feeling her out. I think the tears are happy tears, but I'm not sure.

"It does, Coop. You have no idea. This is…. I have no words. I can't believe you did this for me." She wipes at her cheeks with the backs of her hands.

"Haven't you realized by now I would do anything for you?"

She nods. "I'm in shock. I don't really know what to say to this. I don't know…," she says, shaking her head.

Time to put it all out there. "I was hoping you would want to do this full-time. Run the foundation. I was hoping you would move here with me. That we could buy a house, change your last name, have a couple of kids. What is it they always say? And they lived happily ever after? I want that to be us, Reese. All of it. I want it all with you."

More tears, but an even brighter smile, greets me. "I guess we have some papers to sign."

I kiss her quickly before she moves to her seat, and I get up to open the door, letting John know we're ready for him.

"All right, so this is all the legal filings for the Latham Reeves Foundation."

"Oh my God," Reese says breathily.

"We can change it," I tell her, then look at John for confirmation. "Right?"

"Of course, we would just need to adjust the documents and reprint," he says without an ounce of annoyance. With what I'm paying him, there better not be a sign of any.

Bliss | 143

"No." She shakes her head. "It's perfect."

"Wonderful, let's get started," John suggests.

John takes his time going through each document to explain what we are signing. Reese asks great questions, and they all boil down to one answer. This is her foundation to build and to grow. She smiles the entire time, and she keeps having to wipe the tears from her cheeks.

An hour later, we're walking out of John's office with two folders holding identical information. "I can't believe that you did this," Reese says once we're in my truck.

"Good surprise?"

"The best. Cooper, this is everything I've ever wanted."

"I know. You told me."

"And you listened."

"So, what do you say we grab some dinner since there are no groceries in the house, and we can go home and talk about what our next steps are going to be?"

"Yes," she quickly agrees.

"What sounds good?" I ask, pulling out of the parking lot.

"Anything. I'm starving. Let's do something we can take home with us, though."

"There's a great pizza delivery just down from me. We can call it in now and shouldn't have to wait too long."

"We need beer if we're going to be eating pizza," she replies.

"That's my girl." I turn the truck into the nearest gas station and hand her my phone. "It's under Maurice's. Order whatever you want. You know what I like." I wink and head inside to get my girl some beer.

Chapter 18

REESE

"Why did you let me eat so much?" I ask Cooper. We're sitting on his couch with an open pizza box on the coffee table.

"Told you it was good." He smirks.

"I don't think I can move," I say, trying to lean over and place my now-empty beer bottle on the table. He takes mercy on me and does it for me.

"You want another?"

"No. I'm good. Thanks though."

"All right." He drains his bottle and sets it on the table as well. "Now, we talk." He stretches his legs out beside me and pulls my feet into his lap.

"Honestly, I don't know where to start."

"Let's start with now that it's had time to really sink in, are you upset about the foundation?"

"No. Not even a little. I'm… flabbergasted to be honest. That you would think to do something like that for me."

"I was hoping that would be your response. I know you pretty well, and you've talked a lot about wanting to do more. I can't believe I'm getting ready to say this, but if you want to run the foundation from your apartment, we could make that work. You would just have to come back to Indy for contracts, etc. Everything will be done through John. He's already on retainer for me anyway."

"Isn't that weird for you? That you have an attorney on retainer."

"Yeah." He shrugs. "At first it was really hard to adjust to all the changes, but I've accepted them now and have accepted that while I'm still me, the same old Cooper I've always been, I'm also now a professional football player, and that comes with status and prestige in most cases, and there is nothing I can do to change that."

"You're wrong, Coop. You're making changes. You're changing the world. Look at what you did today. That's amazing. I'm so proud of you and all that you've accomplished. What you did for the kids in the home, that meant everything to them."

"I did it for you, Reese."

I nod. This is my Cooper. The love of my life. The man who created a foundation to make my dreams come true. If this is a dream, I never want to wake up. "So, what are you thinking?" I ask him.

"I told you what I was thinking. I think it's your turn to talk."

"How would this work? I mean, if I give up my job to run the foundation, how am I going to support myself?"

"I assume if I say that I'll support you, that idea's not going to go over so well?" he asks.

"Not particularly. I mean, what would the media think, our parents, and friends?"

"Fuck the media. Our parents and friends have seen this"—he motions between the two of us—"coming for years. It's what we think that matters."

"I don't know, Cooper."

"Fine. The foundation will pay you a salary, just as any foundation would," he concedes.

"But that's taking away from the kids."

"Baby…" He chuckles. "You can't have it both ways. Unless you're leaning toward keeping your job and running the foundation from Columbus."

"You're here." I state the obvious.

"And I want you here with me."

"I want to be where you are," I confess.

"What's mine is yours, Reese. I created this foundation for you and for me. It was with the hopes that not only do you get to do what you've always wanted, reach more people, help more people, it would also bring you home to me."

"Tell me how you see this playing out? Where are we a year from now, five years from now?" I ask.

"Married, and in five years a kid or two."

I get that fluttering feeling in my belly. The one I've come to associate with Cooper. Only he has ever made me feel this way. Thinking of our future, marriage and kids, it's everything I've ever wanted. With him. Only with him. I raise my eyebrows, making him laugh. "How many kids are we talking, Reeves?"

"As many as you want. At least two."

I nod. "I can be on board with that."

"This is what I see and what I want. I want you to give notice and move here with me. I want you living here before I have to leave for training camp. That commute for you to visit on those days will be short, and in the meantime, you can explore the city and dive into the foundation work. I want to come home to you every night, at least those nights that I can. When possible, and your schedule allows, I want you to travel to the games. I want to marry you and have babies with you. Do I need to keep going?" he asks.

"No." I shake my head as I fight back the tears. I've wanted this for so long. Not just everything he just described, but all of it with him. He is my dream, and through his love for me, he gave me mine. No way would I have been able to do all the start-up for a new foundation and get it off the ground holding down a full-time job. Not only that, but he heard me, and without me even knowing, he gave me the perfect career. Loving him and caring for our children as well as those who are vulnerable.

"I have one more question," I say, watching his reaction closely.

"What's that?"

"Will you help me move?" I smile as I say it, but he just sits still, staring at me. There is a blank expression on his face. "Cooper?" I wave my hands in the air to get his attention.

"Shh," he whispers.

"What are you doing?" I whisper back.

"Memorizing the moment."

"So that's a no?" I ask, amused.

"That's a hell fucking yes!" He stands and leans over me, pressing his lips to mine. His tongue traces my lips, and my hand goes around his neck, keeping him close to me. "You're moving here? With me? When?" He fires off questions in between peppering my face with kisses.

"Soon. I need to give notice and pack up my place." Excitement bubbles inside me at this new start. With Cooper. It's everything I could have hoped for, yet it's more. I'm deliriously happy.

"So? A week or so?"

"No, I have to give work at least two weeks." It's going to be hard to leave, but I just need to remind myself of all the kids I'm going to be able to help. I'm so excited to hit the ground running with this new foundation.

"You should do it now. The sooner, the better. Hold on. Let me get my laptop." He stands and rushes down the hall.

"Coop! I'm not going to email them. I'll tell them on Monday!" I yell after him.

He comes back into the room with his laptop. "Fine, but we can start looking at houses." He takes a seat next to me.

"What do you mean, look at houses? I mean, I know you mentioned it, but we live here." I motion around the room.

"You said we." He's grinning like a fool. "You said *we* live here."

"Well, maybe not today, but in a couple of weeks."

"I love you." He leans in and kisses me. "I signed a five-year deal, so we're going to be here for at least five more years. I'd like to be here longer, but we're going to need a house. The kids need a yard to play in, and you need an office to work from home," he rattles on.

"Coop." I place my hand on his arm. "We don't have to do this all at once."

"Yes." He nods. "We do. I've been waiting for this, for us to start our lives together. We're doing this, Reese's Pieces." He winks.

It's been months, hell, maybe longer than just months since he's called me that. That was always his thing, and we lost that, but now we're back. We're better than ever, and it makes my heart happy. We each might have traveled the long road to get here, but I'm confident we'll be traveling it together for the rest of our lives.

"Okay, so what are we looking for?" I ask him.

His eyes light up. "That's my girl." He types something into his laptop and then stops and reaches for his phone. I watch as he dials and places the phone to his ear. "Roger, hey, man, how you been?" he asks. "Listen, I'm ready for the realtor's name. Does she have a website?" I hear him ask. "Thanks, man. Talk soon," he says, ending the call.

"Was that Roger, as in Roger Watters, the quarterback for the Defenders?" My voice is a shrill squeak. How is this our life?

"Yep." He nods as he types. "He bought a house last year and had a great experience with his realtor. This is her site." He turns the laptop so I can see it. He puts his arm around my shoulders and pulls me in close. "Time to find our dream home, baby."

That's how we spend the rest of our night. Scrolling through house listings. It's surreal searching through the homes he's got us looking at. They're huge and fancier than anything I've ever lived in. Cooper says we need to have the best because that's where we'll be raising our family. I argue it's too much money, but he counters that it's our home base and that if we're going to blow money, a home is a good place to do it. He's right, but it seems frivolous.

"Babe, I need you and our future kids to be safe when I'm on the road. These neighborhoods are the best, and most of the houses have gates," he explains when we're lying in bed.

"Okay," I concede. "I can't believe you called the realtor at eleven o'clock at night."

"She was happy to hear from me." He laughs.

"She was happy to think about the potential commission."

"I don't care why. All I care about is that she's making it happen, and we're going to look at houses tomorrow."

"This is unreal, Coop."

Bliss | 149

"This is us, baby. This is our life."

"Thank you for not giving up on me."

"I should be saying that. I know I hurt you, and yet here you are. In our bed, in my arms."

"Nowhere else I'd rather be."

He kisses the top of my head, and I close my eyes. I'm content and happy, and it's hard to believe we're here, but he's right. This is our life, and it's what we make it.

I can't wait to see what our future holds.

"I'm kind of disappointed. I was sure we would have found one we loved by now," Cooper says as we drive to the fourth house of the day.

"They were all nice."

"Yeah, but we didn't love them. I don't want to settle for nice. This is where we're going to be spending the majority of our time, raising our kids, making our kids." He glances over with a quick wink and wag of his eyebrows.

"We have time, Cooper. It's not like your condo isn't nice."

"I know, but I'm ready to do this. I feel like we've been on hold since we were eight. I don't want to be on hold anymore. I want to be full steam ahead in this new life of ours."

I reach over and place my hand on his shoulder. "There's no rush. I'm still moving here as soon as my two weeks are up."

"Damn right you are," he says, pulling into a subdivision.

"Wow, these houses are unreal," I say as I take in each one.

"This is it." He pulls up in front of a wrought iron gate.

We wait as April, the realtor, opens the gate. Cooper follows her through and my breath hitches in my throat. The house sits back off the road, and it's on a small knoll. It's a light brown brick, and it's gorgeous. My favorite of the day by far, but this place has to be out of our price range.

"Welcome." April greets us as we get out of the truck. "Each lot is ten acres or more, so it keeps the neighbors from being right on top of you. There are homeowner association fees that pay for keeping the road maintained. Shall we?" she asks, already heading toward the front door. "You know the drill. I'll be here if you need me. Since this house is empty, you can look around on your own, much like the others. It's five bedrooms, seven bathrooms, and two home offices. There is also a fully finished basement."

"That's huge." I look at Cooper wide-eyed.

"Lots of babies," he whispers, taking my hand and leading me through the house.

With each room we tour, I fall more in love with this place. The kitchen is huge, with a large island and plenty of space to cook and feed a big family or group of friends in our case. The bedrooms are all large, as are the bathrooms and the living area. The master bedroom has a sitting area, and the shower… it's the biggest shower I've ever seen before in my life. Like, ten people would fit in there, comfortably, I might add, all at one time.

"Wow," I murmur when we walk out on the back porch. It's covered, and there is an outdoor kitchen, fireplace, and even a TV. The view of the woods behind the property is so private and serene.

"Good wow?" Cooper asks.

I glance up at him. "It's breathtaking."

"I really like this one, Reese. It's big enough for kids, and we both have an office. There is room for our parents to come and stay when they visit. I really like the theatre room set up in the basement, and this outdoor area… it's private, and I love that. We need that with my career."

"I agree. What did you not like about it?" I ask. I'm hoping he says nothing.

"Nothing. I love it all, and that master bath…." He leans down and places his lips next to my ear. "The things I could do to you in there."

I shiver. "Yeah," I agree.

"What do you think, baby?" He moves to stand behind me, wrapping his arms around my waist. "Can you see us living here? Raising a family here?"

"Can you?" I ask him.

"I asked you first."

"How far away is the stadium?"

"About twenty minutes."

"Not too far of a drive."

"No. In fact, I think a couple of my teammates live close to here."

"So?"

He chuckles. The sound is soft and low, but I can feel the vibration of his chest against my back. "I can see us here."

"Me too," I say excitedly.

"Yeah?"

"Yes."

"Good. Let's go find April." We locate her in the kitchen, leaning over the counter, typing furiously on her phone. "We'll take it," Cooper announces.

"Well, all right then. I'll draw up the paperwork. Can you stick around to sign the offer?" she asks.

"Yes."

"And the price?"

"Full asking. We'd like to move quickly."

"Of course. Give me ten minutes to get this written up, you can sign, and I'll send it over to the seller's agent. Hopefully, we'll hear from them later today."

Fifteen minutes later, we're in the truck headed home. "I can't believe that just happened," I say, scrolling through the picture I took of the house on my phone.

Cooper just grins and reaches over the console for my hand. The drive back to his condo is quiet but not uncomfortable. I can't stop myself from imagining us living there. Excitement like nothing I've ever known races through my veins. It's not the house, as much as it is the meaning of the house.

Our home.

Chapter 19

COOPER

Reese's two-week notice ended up being eight days. She was already scheduled to be off Thursday and Friday of this week for Nixon and Tessa's wedding. They honored that time off, thankfully. She was stressing out about missing the wedding. I tried to assure her it would all work out. I didn't tell her she could just quit. I know Reese, and that's not who she is.

"How was your last day?" I ask her as soon as she comes through the door. She maneuvers herself around the boxes that we've been packing the last two weeks.

"Good. Sad. I promised the kids we'd come back to visit," she says sheepishly.

"Of course we will. Come here." I pull her into a hug. "April just called."

"And?"

"The closing is still on for tomorrow. I moved our flights to early Friday morning."

"Did you tell Nix?"

"Not yet."

She reaches for her phone, hits a few buttons, and it begins to ring. She has it on video, so she holds it out for me to see. "Hey." Tessa smiles on the screen. "Oh, hi, Cooper," she greets me as well.

"Hey, Tess. Where's Nix?"

"Is that Cooper?" I hear Nix ask before his face appears on the screen. "Hey, you two. What's up?"

"Oh, you know, just living the dream. And we bought a house," I say nonchalantly.

"What? You bought a house?" Tessa grins.

"We did," Reese confirms.

"You bought a house together?" Nixon asks.

My hand slides behind Reese's neck as I pull her into a kiss. Just a soft peck on the lips, but Tessa's gasp and Nixon's "about fucking time" tells me it gets the reaction I was hoping for.

"You've been holding out on me." Tessa smiles.

"Kind of. We just wanted to take it slow for a while."

She wanted to take it slow, but I don't correct her. "So we bought a house, and the closing is tomorrow." I drop the bomb.

"No way, man. You are not missing my wedding." Nixon crosses his arms over his chest.

"We're not. We were supposed to fly out tomorrow afternoon, but we changed our flights to Friday morning."

"The rehearsal is at six," Tessa reminds us.

"Our flight lands at one," I explain. "We will be there in plenty of time."

"Good. Now, let's get back to the house. You're living there together? As in roommates or sharing a bed?" Nixon asks.

Tessa nods as if he read her mind. I look over at Reese. "I thought you would have told her?"

"No, I haven't had time to talk to her. She's working, or I'm working." She shrugs.

"She's the love of my life," I tell them.

"Aw." Tessa smiles.

"So the two of you are together, as in an item?" Nixon clarifies. I see the glint in his eyes that tells me he's giving me shit. It's his way of gloating without saying I told you so. I'll take it. I should have listened to him years ago. I should have opened my eyes and tried to see it from his point of view.

"Yes."

"It's about fucking time, my man."

I throw my head back and laugh. We spend the next fifteen minutes chatting and catching up. I assure them we will be there in plenty of time for the rehearsal, and end the call. "You want to head to Indy tonight? The closing is at ten in the morning."

"Yes. That sounds better than getting up at the ass crack of dawn to drive there."

"Maybe we can take some of your things and leave them at the condo," I suggest.

"We'd have to move them twice."

I shrug. "Doesn't matter. We don't have to unpack them, just have them there. Besides, we get the keys tomorrow."

"I can't believe it. Less than two weeks is record time for a house closing."

"It is, but money talks. The title search and appraisal were done quickly, and I paid cash."

"Oh." Her mouth forms the perfect little circle. "Yeah, I guess that will do it."

"We can stay there tomorrow night if we want. It's all ours once we sign those papers."

"Wait," she says with a hint of panic in her voice.

"What?" No way is she backing out on me now.

"Have you told your parents?"

Shit. "No. Have you told yours?"

"No." She chuckles. "Let me grab some clothes and what I'll need for the wedding. If we leave here in thirty minutes, that will get us to their place a little after seven. We can stop in and say hi, give them the news and then head to Indy."

Bliss | 155

"That's going to put us at the condo pretty late."

"Yeah, but we should tell them in person."

"Agreed. Go get what you need. I packed my bag earlier. I laid out some of your stuff I thought you might want on the bed, and your suitcase and carry-on are ready for you too."

"You spoil me," she says, pressing a kiss to my lips.

"Damn right, I do. Get moving, woman." I try to smack her on the ass, but she's too quick as she laughs her way down the hall.

Two hours later, at a few minutes after seven, we're pulling into my parents' driveway. They don't know we're coming. We talked about calling them on the way, but instead, opted to surprise them.

"Are you nervous?" I ask Reese, pulling the keys from the ignition.

"No. Are you?"

"Nope. How do you want to do this?"

"I'll call Mom and Dad and ask them to come over." She pulls her phone out of her purse and dials the call, putting it on speaker so I can hear.

"Reese, what a nice surprise," her mom greets her.

"Hey, Mom. I was hoping you could do me a favor?"

"Anything," she replies.

"Well, Coop and I are sitting in Trevor and Ann's driveway. We were hoping you would come and visit with us for a little while."

"You're here? Now?" she asks. "Garrett, the kids are here!" she yells. "We'll be right there," she says, and the line goes silent.

We get out of the truck and head inside. I don't bother knocking. "Mom, Dad!" I call out.

"Cooper?" Dad asks, appearing in front of us. "Reese." He pulls my girl into a hug. "What are the two of you doing here?"

"We're on our way to my place in Indy. Just thought we would stop in to say hi."

"Aren't you supposed to be on a flight to Louisiana?" Mom asks, hugging us both.

"Yeah, we need to go to my condo first. So we thought we would stop in on our way."

"I'm glad that you did. Reese, we should call your parents," she says, just as there's a knock at the door.

"That would be them," Reese tells her.

The six of us gather in the living room and spend the next twenty minutes or so catching up. It's not until Reese's mom asks about our flights tomorrow that we find our opening.

"You fly out tomorrow, right?" Eve asks.

"Actually," Reese glances at me, "we moved our flights to Friday morning."

"Yeah, we had something come up tomorrow that we had to take care of."

"What's that?" Dad asks, just like I was hoping one of them would.

I look over at Reese, and she's smiling from ear to ear. My girl is happy. Her smile is contagious. Reaching over, I entangle her fingers with mine. "Reese and I bought a house."

The room is silent.

"Did you say that you bought a house?" Garrett asks.

"We did." I'm sure to include Reese in this, because what's mine is hers. She doesn't know it yet, but the house is in both of our names.

"Wow," my dad murmurs. "Where?"

"Indianapolis. About twenty minutes from the stadium."

"You're moving?" Eve asks Reese.

"Yeah. Today was my last day at my job. Cooper…" She swallows hard as her emotions get the best of her. "Cooper started a foundation. The Latham Reeves Foundation." She goes on to tell them all about the foundation. She starts at the beginning, telling them the frustrations with her job, and how I listened and created a solution. She's giving me all the credit, but it's her and her love of helping others… her big heart that she shares with those kids that created this foundation.

By the time she's finished retelling the story, both of our mothers are in tears, and our fathers both wear looks of pride on their faces. "So, we bought a house. Reese is moving to Indy to run the foundation."

"Can we see the house?" Mom asks.

"It's gorgeous," Reese says, pulling out her phone. "I can't believe this is where we're going to be living." She passes her phone around, and they each take turns flipping through the pictures.

"You've done well for yourself, son. I'm proud of you," Dad says.

My chest swells with pride at his words. Sure, I'm good at football, and the money that provides us is going to let us live a life most can only dream of. That's great, but I know it's more than that. He knows Reese is my heart, and he's proud of me for not giving up. For fighting for her. For us.

I nod, accepting his words. However, I keep mine to myself. I don't tell him that I would give it all up for her. If that's what it took for me to spend the rest of my life with her, I'd do it. No questions, no hesitation. I'm glad that's not how it turned out, don't get me wrong, but there is nothing in my life more important than Reese.

"We fell in love with it. It's big enough to start our family and still have room for the four of you when you come to visit."

"Family?" they all four say at the same time.

I dropped that little nugget of information that I know they were all dying to ask but weren't for whatever reason. They've stayed out of our romantic relationship, but it's time they know what's going on. I've told them all that I love her, and this was my plan, but it's time for them to know the plan has been set in motion. Next stop, our engagement and our own wedding.

I look over at Eve and Garrett. Here goes nothing. "I know we've talked about this before," I say, keeping my eyes trained on them. Reese squeezes my hand, I'm sure to get my attention, but I don't break their gaze. "I love her. I want to spend the rest of my life with her. I would like your blessing to do so," I say formally.

Garrett looks over at Eve, and something passes between them. "You're already a part of our family. We'd be honored to officially call you our son."

Our parents gather around us, giving us hugs and congratulations. We talk a little while longer with plans for them to come and see the house when we get back from the wedding. We're barely in the truck with our seat belts on when Reese smacks my arm.

"Ouch." I pretend that she hurt me. She didn't. "What was that for?" I ask, but I already know the answer.

"That—" She points toward the house. "You just did that."

"I did." I fight my grin.

"In front of me and all of them."

"They're our parents."

"I know that."

"They're going to be there when we say our vows. This is nothing new."

"You're acting like we're getting married soon."

"I want to."

"Coop," she breathes.

"Don't worry, tonight wasn't my proposal." She sighs in relief. "Although, you might want to practice your yes."

"What?"

"It's coming, baby. I'm going to ask you one day soon. So you need to work on your yes."

She bites down on her lip to keep from laughing. "What am I going to do with you?" she asks with a shake of her head.

"Marry me, have my babies, grow old with me."

Her smile is huge. "I think we can work something out."

Chapter 20

REESE

"Wow." That's the first thing that comes to mind as Cooper pulls our rental to a stop outside Nixon and Tessa's house. "I've seen pictures, but it doesn't do this place justice." It's similar to ours with a full-brick two-story wrap. Their brick is a dark red, and since red is Tessa's favorite color, I'm sure that's part of what made her fall in love with this place.

"Kind of like our place," Cooper says, peering out the window.

"They are similar. I wonder if they have a huge shower," I say and can feel my face heat. Yesterday after the closing, we went and bought an air mattress before swinging by the condo and grabbing our bags for our flight, our toiletries, and the blankets from Cooper's bed. We ordered Chinese and stopped to pick it up on the way. We spent the rest of the day in our new home. We set up camp in the master bedroom and ate sitting on the island that's the size of my entire kitchen in my apartment.

Anyway, the shower… Cooper insisted we try it out last night, and try it out we did. What started out as soft intimate caresses turned into my back against the wall, with the water raining down on us as he took me hard and fast. Shower sex is definitely on the to-be-repeated-as-soon-as-possible list.

"Just think, babe, that's how we can start every day," he says, reading my mind.

"Promise?"

His reply is to lean in and press his lips to mine. I open for him just like I always do when he deepens the kiss. I allow myself to get lost in him. He's mine now. I can do that. And I do every chance I get. When a loud knock comes at the window, Cooper groans and pulls away. "I love you," he says softly before turning and rolling down the window. "Can I help you?" he asks Nixon and Tessa.

"Get your ass out of the car, Reeves," Nixon demands. I can hear the humor in his voice, or maybe that's excitement for seeing his friend.

Cooper chuckles and climbs out, as do I. As I walk to their side of the car, I see the guys exchange one of those bro-hug things they do. Hands clasped and smacks on the back. Then Cooper lifts Tessa into the air and kisses her cheek.

"Reese." That's the only warning I get before Nixon lifts me in the air and spins me around.

"Put her down, Nix. I need to hug my best friend." I hear Tessa command, and my feet are suddenly back on the ground, only to be engulfed by Tessa. "I'm so glad you're here!" she exclaims.

"Me too." I pull out of her hug, only to be pulled into Cooper's arms. I feel like a yo-yo, but I'm not going to complain. These are my three favorite people. They can hug me all they want.

"How's the house?" Tessa asks as she motions for us to follow her inside.

We head on in, and I can't help but admire the way she's decorated. I can't wait to do that with ours. "We stayed there last night. I feel like I'm living in a fairy tale," I admit, taking a seat on the couch.

"Yeah, I know what you mean," she says, looking around her house.

"It's beautiful, Tessa."

"Thank you. We love it. We looked for weeks before we found this one. As soon as we pulled in, I knew it was the one."

"That's the same thing that happened to me. I could just feel it. I thought I was crazy for thinking that."

"Nope. I was the same way."

"You guys are going to have to come and visit soon." Cooper jumps into the conversation.

"Yeah, you do realize training camp starts almost as soon as we get back from our honeymoon?" Nixon asks him.

"We'll figure it out," Tessa assures them.

"Tell me about the wedding. Is everything all set? What can I help with?" I ask her.

"Everything is set. It's small. Just close friends and family. You know me. I didn't want anything over the top."

"I'm so happy for the two of you. I knew you two were perfect for each other," I boast. "I'm sorry I've not been much help with the planning. I hate that you live so far away."

"She wouldn't let it go," Cooper says from his seat next to me. "She insisted her roommate and mine would be a perfect fit." He points to Tessa and then Nixon. "Now here we are. Congratulations, you two."

"Enough with the heavy," Tessa says, wiping her eyes. There may be tears, but her smile is like a beaming ray of light as she glows with happiness. "I want to see your house."

Not needing to be asked twice, I pull my phone out of my back pocket and show her the pictures.

"I love it." She and Nixon swipe through the pictures.

"Is that an air mattress?" Nixon asks. "Are the Defenders not paying you enough, my man?" he teases Cooper.

"Dick." Cooper laughs, flipping him off.

"Well, once you get back from your honeymoon, you're going to have to come and visit. By then, we'll have furniture for you to sleep on," I assure them.

"Nix leaves for training camp five days after we get back, so maybe then? We can hang out and catch up."

"Yes." I'm excited about the idea of getting to spend some quality time with my best friend.

"Let me show you to your room. Dinner is being catered after the rehearsal, but if you all are hungry, I can make some sandwiches or something."

"I'm good," Cooper says. "We hit a drive-through on the way here."

"I was starving," I tell her.

"Come on." Nixon grabs some of our bags, while Cooper takes the others. "I'll show you to your room."

Cooper and I decide to take a quick nap. We had to be at the airport at five this morning. Stripping down, we slide under the covers curled up in each other's arms. There is no better feeling than being wrapped up in Cooper. We sleep for an hour before it's time to get ready for the rehearsal. I know it's not my wedding, but it might as well be for how excited I am for our friends. To think, I had a part in the two of them getting together, and here we are in their home, the weekend they vow to love each other forever.

I know it's wrong, but I wasn't excited about my wedding to Hunter. I feel like I kind of just went through the motions. My heart flutters in my chest when I think about marrying Cooper. That was definitely missing, and I was wrong for saying yes. I hope Hunter finds a love like ours. He deserves nothing less.

"You're glowing," I tell my best friend. The wedding reception is starting to die down, so the four of us are sitting at a table in the hotel banquet room just enjoying each other's company.

"Damn right, she is," Nixon says, kissing her temple. "My wife is gorgeous," he says, and I melt a little at their exchange. Tessa is smiling at him with tears swimming in her eyes.

"You ready for that to be us?" Cooper whispers in my ear.

"More than you know." What once seemed to be a fantasy is now sitting right next to me. He's mine. Now and forever.

"Me too, baby." He kisses my bare shoulder, which causes goose bumps to break out on my skin. "I hope I can always do that," he says, tracing the bumps on my arms.

I turn to look at him. "There isn't a doubt in my mind."

"What are you love birds talking about over there?" Tessa asks.

"The two of you," I tell her. "Thank you for letting us be a part of your special day."

"You two have been there since the beginning," Nixon comments. "It's fitting that you stood up with us today."

"Maybe one day we can repay the favor?" Tessa says coyly over her glass of champagne.

"Oh, you will," Cooper states confidently. "As soon as I can get a ring on her finger."

"Now we're talking." Nixon holds his fist out for Cooper to bump, making us all laugh.

"Are you excited for your honeymoon?" I ask Tessa. I don't want to make today about Cooper and me. This is their special day. We'll have ours. Soon, I hope.

"Yes! I've always wanted to go to Ireland. I can't wait. Two weeks of nothing but—" she starts, but Nixon interrupts her.

"Sex." He grins.

"There's that." Tessa smiles at her husband. "The landscapes and the cliffs, it looks beautiful. I can't wait to take it all in."

"And the sex," Nixon says, giving her a heated look.

"You're terrible." She giggles.

"Ladies and gentlemen, the last dance of the evening," the DJ announces.

Looking around, it's just the four of us and their parents who are left. The wedding was small and intimate. It was perfect for them in so many ways. "They're calling our name, babe." Cooper stands and holds his hand out for me. We take the dance floor beside Nixon and Tessa, as well as their parents. It's the perfect ending to an even more perfect day.

As my head rests on Cooper's chest and we sway to the music, I let my mind wander to a day just like this. A day where Cooper and I vow to love one another until the end of time.

I used to want a large wedding. I wanted it to be huge and elaborate. When Hunter and I were planning ours, we settled for somewhere in the middle, not huge, but not intimate either. The dreams of my younger self are not my dreams anymore. This moment, the eight of us together, that's what I want for us. I want intimate. I don't need some huge elaborate wedding to prove to him that I love him. Honestly, I would be good with going to the courthouse. I just want to marry him.

I want to marry my best friend.

A few hours later, we're lying in bed, and I can't stop thinking about the wedding. I can't help but imagine what our wedding day will look like. It all plays out like a movie in my mind. A small intimate gathering where the focus is on the love that we share, not the guest list or the decorations. Just us.

I want that.

More than anything, I want to marry Cooper. I've held these feelings close to my chest long enough. I'm ready to start our lives. I know I took longer than I should have to tell him that I love him. I let the fear of heartbreak cloud what was right in front of me. The most amazing man who loves me unconditionally.

"What are you thinking about, babe?" Cooper mumbles. His arms are wrapped tightly around me, as they are every night.

He loves me.

I love him.

It's time.

I roll over to face him. In the dark, I manage to place my hand on his cheek. "You," I whisper.

"What about me?" he asks, pulling me closer. That's the thing with Cooper, he can never seem to get me close enough. He's always reaching for me and touching me in some way. It's not just our hearts that are entangled, it's who we are. My life with his, and I wouldn't want it any other way.

"Marry me." My words are softly spoken, but the intake of breath from Cooper tells me he heard me just fine. "I want our forever, Coop. I don't want to wait to start my life with you. I don't want some big, elaborate wedding. I just need our parents, and I need you. That's it." He doesn't say anything, so I keep going. "I love you. I've never stopped loving you. I'm sorry that it took me so long to say it back. I was scared, and even though you proved over and over again that I was who you wanted, I held back. I'm tired of holding back, Coop. Tonight, watching Tess and Nix, I'm not envious of the love they share. We share that same intense, all-consuming love. What I'm envious of is that they're on their journey to forever. I want to start ours now. Cooper Reeves, will you marry me?"

Once again, I'm met with silence. My mind and my heart are in a battle as they race against one another. The look on his face tells me I've left him speechless. Hot tears prick my eyes when the reality of the moment sets in. I just asked him to marry me. I open my mouth to tell him I was kidding when the bed dips, and I feel the emptiness beside me. The tears begin to fall as the sob that's been lodged in my throat breaks free. I don't know what's happening. This is what we've talked about. "Coop," I whisper his name. Pleading for him to say something.

Suddenly, the room is bathed in a soft glow as the click of the lamp switch echoes throughout the room. Cooper is standing beside the bed, his hands clenched at his sides, in nothing but his boxer briefs. "Come here, baby," he says softly.

I don't want to move. I'm frozen as I watch his throat bob when he swallows. His hands are clenched and although he might be trying to hide it, I see it. The small blue box. More tears stream down my face as realization sets in.

"Reese," he says softly. "Please come here." His voice is laced with tenderness, and love. So much love. Not just in his voice, but in his eyes.

"Fine, we'll do this your way." He grins and shakes his head.

I watch as he walks around the bed and stops next to me. I roll over to face him, wiping my eyes. With one hand, he reaches up and softly strokes my cheek. "You're beautiful," he whispers.

"I'm a mess," I choke. This is not how I imagined my reaction to be at a proposal. Then again, I've never been asked by a man who owns my heart and soul.

Cooper drops to his knees, so we are eye to eye. "I'm so in love with you," he says reverently. "I never knew that a love like ours could exist. I'm merely half a man without you in my life." His large calloused hand cradles my cheek, his thumb wiping at my tears. "It breaks my fucking heart to see these tears." He leans in and kisses the corner of my mouth. "Come on," he says, helping me sit up.

It's really happening. This is a moment I've dreamed of and it's here. I sit on the edge of the bed, my legs dangling over the side, while he kneels before me on the floor. I want to scream and yell and tell him that I asked first, but I hold it all in. I want this moment. All I can do is stare down at him as tears race down my cheeks, and I bite down on my bottom lip.

"Bliss," he says softly. "That's what I feel when I'm with you. There is nothing in my life that even comes close to comparing."

"I- I love you," I manage to say.

"Shh," he murmurs, wiping at my cheeks, one side, then the other. "Let me do this." He gives me a small smile. "When we graduated college, I wanted to ask you to come with me. I didn't because I was so caught up in you following your dreams, and all it did was deny both of us the love we have to share." He takes my hand in his. "I loved you then, Reese. I knew it, and I didn't tell you. Within a week of being without you in my life every day, I knew I fucked up. I knew I was losing the best thing to ever happen to me. I'm sorry it took me so long to pull my head out of my ass."

I can't help but smile at that. "Does that mean your answer is yes?" I smile down at him. "You kind of left me hanging, Reeves."

"That's because you stole my moment." He lifts his left hand that's been at his side this entire time and shows me a small blue box. "I've been carrying this ring around with me for weeks. I wanted to make this huge gesture, something you would always remember. An elaborate proposal for the history books."

My breath stalls in my chest as I stare at the box.

He's stealing my thunder.

He's proposing.

"Breathe, baby," he says as he opens the box. "Did you practice your yes, baby?" He glances at the ring, then smiles up at me.

"I should have told you to work on yours," I say, my smile taking over my face.

He chuckles. It's a deep throaty sound that's uniquely Cooper. "Tonight, I realized that every moment with you is a big memorable moment. I don't need a grand gesture. All I need is you. I will never forget this moment. I will never forget hearing the words will you marry me fall from your lips. I'll never forget how my heart was beating so fast I thought it might beat out of my chest. I will never forget the pure bliss of knowing we are in this life together." He pauses. "Before I go any further, my answer is yes. It will always and forever be yes if it means spending forever with you." I open my mouth to speak, but his index finger to my lips stops me. "I want you to have the same memory, Reese. I want you to remember the words from my lips." He places his hand on my chest over my heart that's racing. "I want you to feel your heart as it beats so fast you feel as though it could beat right out of your chest."

He grins. "Reese, will you do me the incredible honor of becoming my wife? Will you marry me?"

I nod. Over and over again, my head bounces up and down as I struggle to find my voice through the onslaught of emotions. My hand trembles as he takes the ring out of the box and slides it on my finger.

"I need your words, Reese's Pieces," he says, making me laugh.

I swallow hard. "Yes," I say. The words are hoarse with the emotion clogging my throat. "Yes, I'll marry you."

His lips find mine in a bruising kiss, and before I know what's happening, we're on the bed, and he's pushing inside me. He makes love to me like he never has before. Without a doubt, this is a night and a proposal I will never ever forget.

Chapter 21

COOPER

Life has been hectic since my fiancée and I returned home from Nixon and Tessa's wedding. Fuck me, I'll never get tired of calling her that. We moved my fiancée out of her apartment and into our new house. We then moved my condo. We hired movers, but Reese still insisted on packing the boxes ourselves. Then we went furniture shopping. We have a big-ass house and needed a lot more furniture. My *fiancée* wanted us to pick it out together so that while I was away at training camp, it could be delivered, and she could get to work making our house a home.

Speaking of training camp, it's been long and grueling as it always is, but I've missed it. I love the game, and this season I feel invigorated. My rookie season was outstanding, and my five-year contract shows that, but this year still feels different. Instead of wishing Reese were watching, wondering if she was viewing from home, I know my biggest cheerleader will be with me for every game. Maybe not always in the stands, but in my heart. This time, I know I'm in hers as well.

"Cooper!" My name is called out by the media.

It's the last day of camp, and they're swarming as we just wrapped up. I hate this part of the gig, having microphones and cameras shoved in your face. I just have to remind myself that this is my job. It's what I get paid to do.

"Cooper, Harold Johnston, ABN News," he says, stepping in my path. "You've been on fire out on the field. Can you tell us what prompted this? Your stats show you're a gifted player, but the coaching staff seems to be raving about your training camp readiness," he says.

I grin. "I guess that's what happens when everything in your life aligns."

"Meaning?" he asks, shoving the microphone back into my face.

"Meaning, I got engaged during the off-season to my best friend and the love of my life." I shrug.

"Can we get a name?" another reporter yells out.

"Reese." I smile into the camera. "Her name is Reese, and her last name isn't important because she's about to become a Reeves." I grin. Let them chew on that.

"Cooper!" another one yells.

I wave at them and push through the crowd to the locker room. I can only handle so much. I gave them the juicy details that will sell their papers and let the world know that Cooper Reeves is as good as a married man. Besides, I'm going home to see my future wife, and that's what matters.

I rush through a shower, pack my shit, and head home. Pulling up to the gate, I enter the code and drive up our lane. It's damn good to be home. Although this place is still new to us, knowing that this is where she's been laying her head at night, it makes it my home. She's sent me pictures of how she's been organizing and decorating, and I'm excited to see it all in real life. Almost as excited as I am to hold her in my arms and take her to bed.

I've missed my girl.

"Honey, I'm home!" I call out. I hear a screech and then footsteps as they race down the stairs. I barely have time to drop my bag to the floor before she's flying into my arms. I catch her easily as she wraps her arms and legs around me.

"I missed you so much!" she says, burying her face in my neck.

"I missed you too, baby," I say, moving us to the living room, and sitting on the couch that we picked out together.

She pulls back, and her smile lights up her face. "I can't wait to show you everything. Come on." She tries to stand, but I hold tight.

"I want to see it. I promise you, I do. Right now, I just want to hold you."

"How can I argue with that?" she asks, snuggling back up to me.

"Tell me what's been going on?"

"Just getting the house in order. I have all of our things unpacked. The bedroom furniture was delivered, and the bed looks so damn comfortable. I can't wait to sleep in it tonight."

"Where have you been sleeping?" I ask her.

"In my old bed in one of the spare bedrooms. I just didn't feel right that you weren't here." She shrugs.

I kiss her hard, needing her to feel how much I love her. "What else?" I say, panting as I pull away from her kiss.

"I found office furniture that I love, and it was delivered last week. I got it all set up and organized, and I'm ready to dive into the foundation. I've been working with John, and all of the paperwork has been filed and approved. The Latham Reeves Foundation is official."

"You're going to do amazing things, future Mrs. Reeves."

She grins. "Fiji."

"What about Fiji?"

"That's where I want to get married. I just want it to be our parents, and if Nixon and Tessa can make it, that would be great. And anyone you want to be there."

"You. All I want is you. You have my schedule, and you said your Amex arrived, right?" I ask. She nods. "Good. Make it happen. Just tell me when and where, or if you want me to handle it, I can do that too. Just tell me what you need, baby."

"You and me in Fiji."

"How did you come to decide on the location?" I ask, running my fingers through her hair.

"I typed in destination weddings, and it popped up. The images are beautiful."

"How soon can we make this happen?"

"Well, with the season, it's going to be difficult, especially if we want Nix and Tess to be there."

Damn. "So, what you're telling me is that I have to wait until after the Bowl game to marry you?"

"Probably."

"That's too far away."

"It's a few months at best. That will give our parents time to plan to be off work, and us time to plan it all out."

"What do you need from me to make this happen?"

"Nothing. I found an amazing resort. I can show you pictures later. If you like it, I'll call and set it up. Then I just need to tell our families, Nix and Tess, and find a dress."

I can't help but think about the last time she was in a wedding dress and how it all ended. "Do you have one in mind?" I ask her.

"Simple. Elegant. Flowing," she replies wistfully.

"Anything you want, baby. I can't wait to marry you."

"Me too, Coop. Me too."

We spend the next hour talking about life and getting caught up. She tells me more about what she's been up to and her ideas for the foundation, while I tell her about camp and how stoked I am about the team this year. "I really think we have a Bowl team," I tell her. All the guys are on point this season.

"I know you're going to kill it." She kisses my chin. "Now, let's take a tour. I'm dying to show you what I've done while you were gone."

We start in the kitchen as she shows me how she has it all organized, and we go room to room. There are pictures of us from when we were kids to now all through the house, and it tells our story.

"This room," she smiles up at me, "I'm not sure about. If there is anything that you don't like, we can change it."

"I'm sure it's perfect," I say as we stand outside the office that we decided would be mine. "Open the door, Reese. The suspense is killing me."

"Remember, we can change it if you don't like it."

"Baby…." I lean down and kiss her, then pick her up and move her out of the way. As I push open the door, the first thing I notice is the dark mahogany desk that I picked out a few days before leaving for camp. It's all set up with my laptop and a framed picture of us. I recognize it as my first game at CU.

Next, my eyes land on the framed jerseys on the wall. "How did you get all of these?" I ask. My Pop Warner jersey, my high school jersey, the jersey from CU, and now the Defenders. They're all framed and sitting proudly on my office walls.

"Your mom. She had the Pop Warner and high school. I found your CU jersey in some of the boxes I was unpacking, and the Defenders jersey is the one they gave you on draft day.

"The curio cabinet, you might not like, but I wanted to be able to display your achievements. There are going to be so many more I wanted it to be a safe place to display them." She points to the cabinet sitting in the corner.

It's filled with the trophies of my youth, all the way through college. There are ring holders sitting on the top shelf. One with my three college rings and another sits empty. "What's up with the empty one?" I ask her.

"Future Bowl ring."

I walk to where she's standing just inside the door and press my lips to hers. "It's perfect, Reese. Thank you for doing all of this."

"I enjoyed it." She slides her arms around my waist. "Let's go see the rest of the house."

We head to the basement where the theatre room is set up, and the pool table has been delivered. "I didn't do much down here. I just pointed to where you wanted everything and figured you could make this man cave how you want it."

"I think we need a poker table," I tell her, and she nods. "Yeah, I thought you might say that. And you're going to need to stock the bar." She indicates to where the new bar and stools sit in the corner by the small kitchenette.

"Now the upstairs," she says. With my hand in hers, she guides me back up to the main level of the house and then up the stairs. "I used our beds to make two spare bedrooms for now, for when we have guests. The furniture in our room is here, and I love it," she says excitedly.

We stop at each room so I can see what she's done, and there are two empties. I wonder how long she wants to be married before we start working on our family? I don't have a chance to ask her as she leads us into the master bedroom, and I take it all in. The huge king-size four-poster bed we ordered is positioned in the center of the room. The matching dressers and nightstands complete the look. At the foot of the bed is the TV that rises when we're watching and then slides back into the deep mahogany wood case that it's housed in when we're not. We splurged a little on that, but I wanted this room to be perfect.

It's our sanctuary.

"All of your clothes are in that dresser or hung up in your closet," she says from where she stands next to me.

I turn to look at her. "I love this, and I love you. You are what makes this place a home, Reese." My lips touch hers. It's meant to be brief, but it's anything but. Within minutes, we're both stripped of our clothes, and I make love to her for the first time in our new bed. We nap and make love all afternoon, and it's my new favorite thing to do.

Chapter 22

REESE

It's game day. The first home game of the regular season. Cooper's parents and mine are here staying with us. It's also the first time they are getting to see our house. They all fell in love with it. Cooper and our dads spent some time in the basement playing poker while Mom, Ann, and I sat around catching up.

"I'm glad our parents are coming today," Cooper says.

We're lying in bed watching the clock. He has to leave soon for the stadium. We had breakfast with everyone, and as soon as the kitchen was cleaned up, Cooper pulled me upstairs with him. He climbed into bed, and I followed. This is where we've been ever since.

"Me too. Although, don't you think it's a little rude that we just left them down there?"

"No. They've been here for four days, Reese. We've spent time with them. I just needed some me and you time before I leave."

"It's a home game," I remind him. "You'll be coming home to me tonight."

"I know. I can't explain it even if I tried." He sighs heavily. "Last season I was a mess. All I could think about was you, and missing you. This time it's different. I just need to hold you a little longer. I know you're going to be there, but I just needed this time with you."

"I'm not complaining," I say, pulling him into a kiss. "I did think you dragged me up here for sex. I wasn't expecting teddy bear Cooper."

"Teddy bear Cooper?"

"Yeah, you know, when you want to cuddle and be all sweet."

"As opposed to?"

"Sexy Cooper."

"Sexy Cooper?" He laughs.

"Yeah, you know, when you get all growly and demanding."

"You think I'm sexy?"

"You know I do."

"What about when we're making love?" he asks, kissing my neck. "What am I then?"

"Mine." I breathe the words as his teeth nibble at my ear.

"Good answer, baby."

My eyes glance over at the clock, and I know he has to go or he's going to be late. "Coop, you need to get going."

"I know," he says, resting his forehead against my shoulder. "I'll see you after?"

"We kind of live together, so it's a sure thing," I tease.

"Thank fuck for that." He rolls out of bed and saunters into the bathroom. Ten minutes later, he appears with his bag in his hand. "Walk me out."

I nod and follow him downstairs. The sound of our parents talking carries up from the basement. "They sound like they're having a good time," I comment.

"They do. I'm glad they're here." We walk out into the garage, and he kisses me soundly. "I left something for you. It's hanging in your closet."

"Babe, have you seen my closet? That will be like finding a needle in a haystack."

"Trust me, you'll find it." With another quick kiss, he climbs in his truck and pulls out of the garage. I hit the button for the door, and head back inside to find my gift and to get ready.

Walking into the closet, my eyes scan, and I stop when I see a Defenders jersey. Pulling it off the hanger, I take a look. It's just like the one I already own, that is until I flip it to the back. Instead of REEVES on the back, it says *MRS. REEVES*. At the top, in small cursive letters, the word *Future* is added. I'm all smiles as I pick up my phone and dial his number.

"Miss me already?"

"I found my present."

"And?"

"Don't you think it's a little over the top?" I ask.

"Nope. You are my future wife, are you not?"

"Yes."

"I want the whole damn world to know it, Reese. I'll be looking for you in the stands, the media is going to be looking for you after my comment that's been on every damn sports station. I want them to know who you are. I want them to know that you're mine."

How do I say no to that? "Well, all right then."

He laughs. "Love you. I'll see you soon."

"Love you too. Have a great game."

"You're going to be there, you know I will," he replies, and the line goes dead.

Sliding my Defenders jersey that I already had on off, I put on the new one. I glance in the mirror at my reflection. I'm wearing jeans that are ripped in the knee, tennis shoes, and my jersey. My hair is pulled up in a ponytail, and I plan on sporting my Cooper Reeves Defenders hat. I look like any other fan who's going to be in that stadium today. Everything except for the five-carat diamond ring adorning my left hand, and the jersey claiming me as his.

Grabbing my hat from where I left it on the nightstand, I pull it on and snap a picture front and back using the mirror and send them to Cooper.

Cooper: My girl.

Smiling like the fool in love that I am, I slide my phone into the back pocket of my jeans and head downstairs to find our parents.

"And the Defenders take home a win!" The announcer's voice echoes throughout the stadium.

"They're kicking off this season with a bang," his co-anchor agrees.

"That they are. Fans, stick around and keep your eyes on the jumbotron screens at either side of the stadium for interviews from your favorite players," they inform the crowd.

"Oh, he hates this part," I tell our parents. Cooper got us amazing seats, right on the fifty-yard line. We had our choice of one of the private booths, but all five of us said we wanted to be in the crowd in the action.

"Excuse me." I turn to look over my shoulder. "I saw your jersey," a woman says. "My son is a huge fan of Cooper's. Would it be possible to get your autograph?" the woman asks sweetly.

"Uh, sure." I smile. Glancing over at our parents, I shrug and turn to face them. She hands me a Defenders T-shirt.

"Anywhere is fine," she says, handing me a black Sharpie. Turning the shirt over in my hand, I see Cooper's name scrawled across the number. "He signed it before the game," the mom explains.

With shaking hands, I poise the Sharpie to sign my name when an idea hits. Instead of my full name, I sign *Future Mrs. Reeves*, and Cooper's number underneath. I hand the shirt to the little boy. "Here you go, buddy."

"Thanks, Mrs. Reeves," he says, smiling wide.

My heart flutters in my chest. I'm going to be Mrs. Reeves. My grin is infectious as I look over at our parents, who are also smiling as they watch me. I can feel my face heat, but I own in. I'm happy. My heart is happy. Cooper and I have fought a long hard fight to be where we are, and I'm going to enjoy every damn minute of it.

"Cooper, great game out there today." A female reporter stops him.

His smiling, sweaty face appears on the screen. "Thanks."

"Two touchdowns, on a three-touchdown winning game, how does it feel?"

"It feels good to bring home the first win of the regular season. My teammates and I have worked hard for this, and we all showed up to play."

"Rumor has it you got engaged in the off-season," she comments.

Again, I can feel my face heat. It feels as though the eyes of all those around me are focused on me and not Cooper. I don't dare look. Instead, I keep a smile plastered on my face, red cheeks and all, and keep my attention on the screen where my man is surely about to embarrass me even more.

Cooper's smile lights up the entire stadium. "The rumor is true. I'm marrying my best friend."

"Does this friend have a name?" the reporter asks.

"Future Mrs. Reeves." He grins cheekily.

The reporter smiles at him, and then something in her features changes. I can't describe it, and I don't have time to because she opens her mouth, and the words she speaks has bile rising up in my throat. "Rumor also has it that she left her fiancé at the altar for you. How well do you know the future Mrs. Reeves?" she asks smugly.

The smile drops from his face, and I know he's pissed. I can see it in the tic of his jaw and the look in his eyes. "Let's get something straight right now. Reese is my best friend. She has been since I was eight years old. Yes, she was engaged before, and it never happened. That's all that you need to know. I love this team, the Defenders is my home, but I promise you that I will not stand for you or anyone portraying her in a bad light. I suggest you take this as your one and only warning." He then looks up at the camera. "To anyone else out there who thinks they can run me and my fiancée through the mud to sell papers, I advise you to think again. I know you're aware of my new contract with the Defenders, and I'm prepared to spend it all to defend her honor." He gives the camera a hard look, then moves to bestow the same look on the reporter before he runs to the sidelines just below where we are sitting and jumps the wall.

I stand still, frozen, waiting to see what happens next. All attention is suddenly on him as he stands before me. His hand lifts to my face, and he smiles down at me. It's the smile I get from him every day. The one that says he loves me, and he always will. "Hey, beautiful," he says softly.

"Coop, I'm so sorry, I—" I start, and he cuts me off with his index finger to my lips.

"No, baby. I'm sorry. My job brought this on you, and I promise you I will fight any story. Hell, I'll give it all up if I have to. I won't let them talk to you or treat you like that."

"Nothing they say can hurt me. The only thing that can hurt me is losing you."

His eyes soften. "That's never going to happen, Mrs. Reeves."

"Future," I remind him, smiling.

"I love you," he says, shaking his head.

"I love you too."

He leans in and kisses me, and the crowd goes crazy. We pull away from the kiss and look around to see that we are now on the jumbotron. Cooper raises my engagement ring to his lips and places a kiss there before releasing me and jumping back over the wall.

My mom loops her arm through mine as I stand here and watch him jog off to the locker room with the rest of his team. I don't want to turn around to face the crowd, but I know that I have to.

"Ready?" I turn and lean out a little to look at our parents.

"Uh, Reese." Trevor smiles. "I think you should turn around."

"Why? Are they all staring at me?"

"Just do it, sweetheart," my dad says.

Mom and Ann grin and nod, as Mom drops her arm from mine. Taking a deep breath, I turn, and tears prick my eyes. There is a line formed, but not to exit the stadium. No, it's formed, waiting for me.

"He's my favorite," a teenage boy says, who is first in line. He takes the hat off his head and hands it to me with a Sharpie. "Will you sign this?"

I nod, unable to speak from the knot in my throat. I sign *Future Mrs. Reeves* with Cooper's number and hand it back to him. The next person steps up, and I repeat this same step over and over again. It's surreal, and these are his fans. I can't turn them away. They're showing their support for him and for me. I was scared of being judged by his fans, by the media, but here on his home turf, this is their way of telling me they don't care about my past, only our future. They support their favorite player and, by association, me.

I stand here with our parents at my side and sign every item placed in front of me. There are maybe ten people left in line when Cooper appears. He shakes hands, and signs items sent his way, and when he makes it to me, he pulls me into his side.

"Looks like you have some fans."

"They're your fans." I smile up at him.

"You better get busy so we can go home." He nods, and to my surprise, the ten or so people are still there. I figured once they got his signature, they would leave, but they stayed. I take the seat cushion and sign what I've been signing all day.

"That's fucking awesome." Cooper grins when he sees it.

I laugh, not looking at him, and sign the next item given to me. Once they are all gone, I turn to look at our parents and Cooper, who are watching me. All five of them are smiling. "What?"

"It's a good thing you aren't the one with the professional career. You'd never be able to leave the house." Ann chuckles.

"Why?"

"Because you can't tell them no. I don't know of anyone, even me, who would have stood there that long to sign autographs," Cooper explains.

"But they're your fans, and they support us. I thought that was the least I could do."

"The media is going to love her," Trevor comments.

"America's power couple. I can see it now," my dad replies dramatically.

"Come on, you goofs. I'm starving."

"Let's go home." Cooper takes my hand in his and leads us up the steps and out of the stadium. The six of us head back to our place. The guys throw some steaks on the grill, while Mom, Ann, and I make some sides. It's the perfect ending to a day I thought was going to end in disaster.

Bliss | 183

Chapter 23

COOPER

It's the week before Thanksgiving, and the Defenders have a bye this week. You know who else has a bye? The Louisiana Badgers. That means that Nixon and Tessa are free. Reese and I are free. Our parents made themselves free when I called them last week.

I don't want to wait until February to marry Reese. I need her to be my wife now. As in this week. She already has a dress; it's at her parents' place. Her mom is bringing it with her. She sent me a picture of it in her luggage. Tessa, Mom, and Eve have helped me so much with this little plan of mine. I owe them. Mom and Eve assured me they knew what Reese wanted me to wear and after rattling off my measurements, they're taking care of it. That was last week, and I'm not worried. I know they will come through for me. For us.

Our parents, as well as Tessa and Nixon, are already on a flight to Fiji. They're taking care of everything; the hard part is getting my gorgeous fiancée there without her knowing what's going on. I have a plan for that as well. I'll just have to see if I can pull it off.

Speaking of my fiancée, she's currently still sleeping peacefully. We don't have to rush; our flight doesn't leave until later this afternoon. I thought that was best in case I need to do some convincing. Careful so as to not wake her, I push her hair out of her eyes. Leaning in, I kiss her forehead and pull her a little closer. I can never seem to get her close enough.

"Morning," she says, slowly blinking her eyes open.

"Morning, beautiful."

"What's got you so chipper?" she asks over a yawn.

"Bye week."

She smiles. It lights up her face and warms my heart.

"You still have practice and stuff, though, right?"

"We do, but Coach is giving us a couple of days off to rejuvenate before we get back to it. We don't play again until next weekend."

"I'm so excited to get some time with you."

"Yeah?"

"You searching for compliments, Reeves?" she teases.

"Nope. But I do have an idea."

"Oh, yeah? What's that?" she asks, snuggling up to me.

"I was thinking, we should go check out the resort where we're going to get married. Make sure the pictures do it justice. I don't want to get there, and the place be a shitshow." I know it's not, and so does she, but this is the best I could come up with.

"The pictures are nice, and the reviews are great. I think we're okay."

"Just humor me then. I still want to go. We can't stay long since I have to get back for practice, but it would be nice to go away with you for a couple of days. We've never done that. Just the two of us."

"That does sound nice. I wonder if we can even get a flight, and it would cost a fortune."

"We can afford it," I assure her. "Let me look." I grab my phone from the nightstand and pretend to search for flights while she uses the restroom. I pull up my ticket confirmation email and scroll to where she can't see the date it was sent, and I'm ready. "Done," I say when she steps out of the bathroom.

"What do you mean, done?" she asks.

"I mean there were two first-class seats this afternoon. We have to be at the airport by noon. Our flight leaves at one thirty."

"You booked it?"

"Yep." It's always better to ask for forgiveness instead of permission; at least, it is in this case.

"Coop, this is crazy. We can't just fly to Fiji."

"Sure we can. You better grab a shower and pack a bag. We're only going to be there for three days, so pack light." Not that she's going to need much. Everything she needs for the wedding is there, and I don't plan on getting dressed any time after we say *I do*. At least not until we have to go home.

"You're serious?"

"Yes. I'm going to grab a quick shower and make us some breakfast."

"You need to pack."

"I know, but I'll just toss some shorts and whatnot into a bag. I'm a guy. I'm easy. Besides, I don't plan on us needing much clothing, if any." I wink at her.

"Where are we going to stay?" she counters. "We can't just fly to Fiji without a reservation."

"It's an all-inclusive thing. I booked it with one of those online deals that give you the flight, the room, and the car at one price."

"We're really doing this?"

"We are, so get that fine ass of yours in gear." I climb out of bed and drop a kiss to her lips on my way to the shower. "Don't come in here. Give me five minutes. If we shower together, we're never going to make our flight." Damn tempting woman.

"I'll start packing," she says excitedly.

I'm grateful my back is to her so she doesn't see my smile. Convincing her that this was a good idea was a hell of a lot easier than I thought it would be. My plan is coming together and tomorrow evening, as the sun sets—just as she planned it—we'll vow to love each other for eternity in front of those who are closest to us.

I can't fucking wait.

"I tried to call my mom and yours to let them know we were going out of town, but I got their voice mail," Reese says from her spot next to me. We just made it through security and are sitting at the gate, waiting to board our flight.

"Did you leave them a message?"

"Yeah, that's just odd that neither of them answered," she says, staring down at her phone.

"It is in the middle of the day, and they are working," I remind her.

"I know, but usually they always take my calls."

"Spoiled," I tease her.

"Hush." She laughs, leaning her shoulder into mine.

"We can call them when we land. I'm sure they're both going to want to hear all about the resort." It's not a lie. We can call them when we land. She just doesn't know they're going to be in Fiji when she calls them. This plan is coming together so smoothly. I keep waiting for some kind of hiccup, but so far, everything is falling right into place.

"True. I'm really excited to see it. This was a great idea. Frivolous, but a great idea all the same."

"This is our wedding we're talking about. I want this day to be everything you ever dreamed it would be. It's worth the trip to make sure that happens."

"We're getting married." Her smile lights up my life.

"Damn right we are. It can't happen soon enough," I say, kissing the corner of her mouth.

"How pissed do you think our families would be if we got married while we were there?" she asks.

I turn in my chair to look at her. "What are you saying?"

She shrugs. "Just a thought. I mean, it's where we want to get married, and we're going to be there. It's what we both want. We're only waiting because of your schedule. I didn't know you would get time off during your bye week, or I would have scheduled it for this week anyway."

I'm flabbergasted by what she's saying and fucking thrilled at the same time. This little surprise I have planned is going to be well received. That just lifted a huge weight off my shoulders.

"I mean if you don't want to—" she starts, but my kiss stops her from saying anything else.

"There is nothing I want more in this life than for you to be my wife."

"Don't say no," she says, with a hint of pleading in her voice. "Just keep an open mind when we get there. See how we're both feeling about it then."

"You really want to do this? Get married without our families?"

She shrugs. "It's not ideal, but the truth is, I want to be Mrs. Reeves. Maybe we can have another small ceremony or something after the season is over. Hell, we could even come back here. You could marry me twice." She grins.

"Baby, I would marry you every single fucking day." I press my lips to hers.

When she pulls away, she whispers once more, "Just think about it."

I nod. I was stoked about this trip before, and now even more so. There was some worry she wasn't going to be ready, but she's eased my fears.

I'm excited for when we land, and she sees our parents, Tessa, and Nixon. She's going to go crazy, and I can't fucking wait.

We board our flight, and I fight the battle of my surprise getting the best of me. I want to tell her now what's about to happen. I manage to keep my shit in check and not spoil it for her, but the suspense is killing me. I can't wait to see the smile that lights up her face when she realizes what I've done.

Even more than that. Tomorrow at this time, she's going to be Mrs. Cooper Reeves. It's been a long time coming. A year ago, this felt so out of reach for us, but now, here we are, and I'm never letting her go.

Never.

Chapter 24

REESE

Sixteen hours later, we've reached our final destination. That was a long-ass flight, but the view before me as we ride to the resort is breathtaking. Instantly, I know it feels right. This is where we are meant to vow to love one another until death do us part. I just hope I convince Cooper to do it this trip instead of waiting. I'm tired of waiting. I'm ready to move forward to start our life, and what better time than now?

Sure, I wish our families could be here, but it is what it is. The marriage is about us. Me and Cooper and the love we share. They'll understand. They all know the battle it's been for us to get here. They know what's in our hearts, and I'm certain they will be thrilled for us.

"So, have you thought anymore about getting married?"

"Every fucking day."

"How about today? Or we could do tomorrow?" I offer sweetly.

"You really want to marry me. Here and now?"

"Yes." I don't hesitate with my answer. This is what I want. Here. Now. Forever. I want to be his.

"Your destination," the driver says, interrupting us.

"Thank you." Cooper reaches up to pay him, including a hefty tip, and we climb out of the car.

"Wow." I look around, and my eyes land on the sign. "Coop! This is it. This is the place I wanted to get married." It's fate, it has to be.

"Is it?" he asks.

"Yes. See, it's official. It has to happen. This is not a coincidence."

He pulls our bags from the trunk and wheels them behind him. I follow, soaking in the beauty that surrounds us. Cooper checks us in, and I follow him to the elevator.

"I got us the largest suite they have. Might as well see what it's all about," he says, smiling.

"I love you."

His brown eyes sparkle. "I love you more."

The elevator dings and we walk down the hall to our room. "Babe, the key is in my back pocket," he tells me.

I fish it out and open the door, holding it for him. "Go on in," he says, propping it open with his foot.

I turn around and am greeted with a chorus of "Surprise." I stop in my tracks as I take in Nixon and Tessa first. Her smile is wide as she winks at me. Then it's Trevor and Ann. She's wiping tears from her eyes while Trevor is smiling widely. Finally, I come to rest on my parents. My mom is crying and my dad, well, he's smiling just as wide, if not bigger than Trevor.

"What? I don't understand," I say, my eyes scanning back over the six of them. I turn to look at Cooper and find him on one knee.

"I love you." His voice is strong. Confident. "I can't wait any longer. I took a risk changing things on you, but I promise we've done everything that we can to make this day exactly as you planned. Reese." He swallows hard. "Will you marry me, baby? Here. Now, in Fiji?"

Tears coat my cheeks as I struggle to take in a breath. That's what he does to me. My fiancé. He takes my breath away. Never in a million years was I expecting this. We're getting married. Here. Now. "Yes!" I say excitedly. I've kept him waiting long enough. I don't want to wait until the season is over. I thought we had to. This is perfect. I'm ready to be his wife. I'm ready for him to be my husband. I'm ready to start the next phase of our lives together.

He stands and pulls me into a kiss, and our family swarms us. Breaking apart, we accept hugs and handshakes before settling in the sitting area.

"I have to know. How did you pull this off?" I ask all of them.

"It's all that man of yours," Tessa explains. "He called us last week and put the plan in motion."

"You have a bye week too?" I ask Nixon, which is obvious, or he wouldn't be here.

"Yep."

"Why didn't I realize that sooner? I could have planned this week."

"You did," Cooper tells me. "I called the resort, and they assured me everything you had planned for our February date would be possible this week as well."

"I brought your dress," Mom adds.

"And I have Cooper covered," Ann tells me.

"You've all thought of everything."

"We have," Mom, Tessa, and Ann say in unison.

"So, when is this going down?" I ask, unable to hide my grin of excitement.

"Tomorrow," Cooper says, kissing my temple. "You and the ladies will stay here, while the guys and I have the suite next door."

"Don't worry," Tessa assures me. "You'll have a suite of your own after tonight." She wags her eyebrows, and my face flushes with heat.

"There are four suites on this floor, and we have them all. But our mothers and Tessa thought that a girls' night and a guys' night, kind of like bachelor and bachelorette parties, would be fun."

I take a minute to let all this soak in. Everyone I love is here to make this happen for us. "I can't believe we're getting married," I squeal.

"Believe it, baby," Cooper whispers.

"All right. Everyone, go get rested up. I'm sure the two of you want to shower and take a nap after that long flight," Mom says.

"When did you all get here?"

"Yesterday," Dad replies. "We've had a day to get rested. Now you two do the same, and we're going to make sure everything is good to go for tomorrow."

"Meet back here at five," Tessa announces.

After another round of hugs and handshakes, they filter from our room to theirs. "Coop." I breathe his name.

"Yeah, baby?"

"I can't believe you did this."

"I would do anything for you, Reese."

I slide my hands under his shirt and reach for the button on his shorts. "Oh,

no you don't," he says, removing my hands and taking a step back.

"What?" I ask coyly.

"The next time I'm inside you, it will be when you're my wife."

"Are you serious?"

"As a heart attack. Just think about the tension that will build and the release of knowing that we're making love as husband and wife."

"Who knew you had all this sweetness in you, Reeves?"

"Only for you, my future wife. Only for you."

Girl time consisted of facials, manicures, and pedicures at the resort spa. Cooper managed to recreate the wedding I had planned. Sure, the resort helped them, but the fact that they did this, all of this, brings tears to my eyes.

"I can't believe you're getting married," my mom says a few hours later back in my suite. The four of us are sitting around, relaxed, and drinking a glass of wine.

"We've talked about this for years," Ann agrees.

"So have I. I could tell within a minute of being around the two of them I knew we'd end up here someday," Tessa says proudly.

"You did not." I point at her.

"Okay, maybe not for certain, but I knew you loved each other and were afraid to admit it."

"But look at you now." Ann holds her glass of wine in the air. "To love. To the little girl, who stole not only my son's heart but his father's and mine as well. Reese, you have always been a part of our family, and I couldn't be happier that I finally get to call you my daughter for real."

"Damn you," Tessa says, wiping tears from her eyes, making us all laugh.

"How's married life?" I ask, trying to lighten the heavy.

"Not much different than life before. Although, I will admit that changing my name has taken some getting used to."

"Reese Reeves," Mom says, trying it out. "It has a ring to it."

"Right?" Ann agrees.

"I feel like I'm living in a fairy tale. Who gets whisked away to Fiji to find their best friend and their family there for a surprise wedding?"

"You do," the three of them echo.

"I knew that when he finally realized what was in front of him all along, he was going to be all in. That's how Cooper is. Look at what it's done for him and football," Ann tells us. "He loves the game and gave it his all, getting him where he is today. I knew he would be the same with you, Reese. I've never seen him this happy."

"Or sappy," Tessa rhymes. "That man has given you his balls." She snickers.

"Tess!" I scold, laughing.

"Oh, we know," Ann assures us.

"Eep! I'm getting married!"

We dissolve in a fit of laughter that carries us through the rest of the night. We finally decide we should get some sleep around midnight. I just snuggled under the covers when my phone rings. I rush to answer it, knowing it's Cooper.

"Hey," I whisper.

"I miss you."

"This was your idea," I remind him.

"I know. What the fuck was I thinking?"

"You were being romantic."

"Yeah?"

"Definitely."

"Tomorrow, Reese's Pieces. Tomorrow you'll be my wife."

"I can't wait."

"You have no idea."

"We should get some sleep," I tell him. "We have a big day tomorrow."

"I don't think I'm going to be able to sleep," he admits.

"We should try," I say, aware it will be hard for me as well.

"I just needed to hear your voice."

"Goodnight, Cooper. I love you."

"Goodnight, babe. I love you too." The line goes quiet, but neither one of us hangs up.

"Coop." I laugh. "We have to get some sleep."

"Good idea. Let me in."

"What?"

"I'm outside your door. Open up and let me in."

"I can't do that. This was your idea."

"Cooper!" I hear Ann's voice. "Get to your room," she scolds him.

"Mom, I'm a grown man." He laughs at her.

"And I'm still your mother. Leave that girl alone. You'll see her tomorrow." There is some rustling, then her voice comes on the line. "Goodnight, Reese," she says, and the line goes dead.

I chuckle as I close my eyes and try to tamp down my excitement to fall asleep. *Tomorrow, I'm getting married.*

To my best friend.

Chapter 25

COOPER

I'm standing in my parents' suite, trying not to watch the clock. Not that I need to watch it. I'm counting down the minutes, the seconds until she walks out on the beach to me. To our forever. I'm sporting my firmly pressed khaki pants and white button-down with the sleeves rolled up to my elbows. That was a specific request that Tessa stressed. Something about forearms and veins. I didn't ask, just did as I was told. I want this day to be exactly what Reese wants it to be.

"You nervous?" Nixon asks.

"Nope. Were you?"

"Not even a little. I knew Tess was the love of my life. The wedding was just a formality."

"Pretty much."

"I know I've given you a lot of shit about Reese, but I'm glad the two of you are finally on the same page. She's good for you."

"I couldn't agree with you more. You can say I told you so. I deserve it."

"Nah, not today. It's your wedding day, but you can bet your ass I'll be saying those four words to you a lot." He grins.

"You boys ready to get this show on the road?" Dad asks.

"Yeah, where's Garrett?"

"He's with Reese, getting ready to walk her down the aisle."

I smile. I can't help it.

"Come on, Romeo." Nixon laughs, placing his hand on my shoulder.

The three of us make our way out to the beach. It's a private section that the resort allowed us to use as our own, just for the service. It's blocked off, and I appreciate the privacy. That's another perk of getting married here this week. The media didn't have time to catch wind of it, and the day is ours. All ours. I know as soon as we get home, word is going to spread. In fact, I want it to. I already talked to Mary, and she's going to release a public statement about me marrying the love of my life, my best friend in a private ceremony. It's all penned and ready to be released. Soon, the entire world will know she's my wife. All I can say to that is it's about fucking time.

I stand at the arch that is covered in flowers. Nixon stands behind me. My mom and dad are sitting on one side of the aisle, while Eve sits on the other with an empty seat for Garrett. I stare at the small gathering of palm trees. I'm told that's where she's going to be coming from. I dig my toes in the sand, my bare feet feeling the warmth of the grains as I talk myself out of going after her.

With the backdrop of the ocean waves behind us, Tessa finally appears. Her dress is a light teal color. It's short, just above her knees, and flowing. It's sleeveless, and by the intake of breath from my boy behind me, she's breathtaking. She's beautiful, but she's not my Reese. I watch as she only has eyes for her husband, tossing him a wink before taking her spot standing across from us.

My parents and Eve stand, and it's showtime. My eyes are glued to the palms as she appears, with her arm looped through her father's. It's now my turn to lose my breath as it falters in my chest at the sight of her. Her hair is pulled back at the base of her neck, and there are loose strands blowing in the wind. Her dress... fuck me, that dress. It's long and flowing from the waist down, reminding me of a ball gown. From the waist up, it's lace and beads and sheer material that has me swaying on my feet. It's fastened around her neck, and already I'm imagining taking it off her.

This time will be different.

This is our wedding.

She is my wife.

My wife.

I don't take my eyes off her as Garrett leads her to where Tessa, Nixon, and I stand. She's within reaching distance, but I know I can't reach for her. Not yet. He has to give her to me. That's how this works. She will forever, from this day forward, be mine.

"Ladies and gentlemen, we are gathered here today," the officiant begins. He drones on until he reaches the question I've been waiting for. The one that will get her closer to me. The one that will make us two "I dos" away from her being my wife. "Who gives this woman to this man?" he asks.

Garrett stands tall. "Her mother and I do," he says, and I pull my hand from my pocket and hold it out for her. With a kiss to her cheek, he places her hand in mine, and Reese steps in front of me.

"You," I say, swallowing hard. "You take my breath away," I say, literally finding it difficult to pull breath into my lungs. This day that I wanted and waited for for so long, I can't believe it's finally here.

I'm so focused on Reese that I don't notice that Garrett is still standing with us. I turn to look at him, and tears swim in his eyes. "I'm not going to tell you to take care of her, I know that you will. I'm not going to tell you to love her forever, because I know that goes without saying. I would like to make it known that today, I'm not just giving her away." He gives me a knowing look. "I'm placing her heart in the hands of a man who I know will love her almost as much as I do." He winks. "I've watched you love my little girl since she was that, a little girl. I'm so proud of both of you and wish you nothing but love and happiness. Love each other. Take care of each other." He swallows hard. "I'm gaining a son today. A man I'm proud to welcome into our family."

I nod, biting on my lip to keep my emotions in check. Garrett steps forward and offers me his hand.

"Thank you, sir." It seems fitting even though he's been Garrett to me from day one. Today it's a special day.

"Welcome to the family, son." He pulls me into a one-armed hug. It's quick but no less powerful before he pulls away and takes his seat next to his wife.

I take Reese's hand in mine once again and give her all my attention. Tears are sliding over her cheeks, and she's doing nothing to stop them. Reaching up, I wipe them with my thumbs. "I love you."

She smiles through her tears. "I love you too."

I get lost in her green eyes as the ceremony continues. I feel Nixon tapping my shoulder, and I pull out of my trance that is my bride, and look at him. He's holding out her wedding band. I shrug and turn back to Reese, who is laughing, as is everyone else. That's what she does to me. Consumes my world. We exchange rings and say our "I dos" and the moment I've been waiting for arrives.

"I now pronounce you husband and wife, you may—" I don't wait for him to tell me. I slide my arms around her waist and pull her into me. I kiss her soft and slow, just what the moment asks for. Tonight, in our room, behind closed doors, that's when I'll kiss her like my life depends on it. That's when I'll take my time removing this sexy-as-hell dress from her body and worship her.

My wife.

Forcing myself to pull out of the kiss, I entangle her fingers with mine as we turn to face our parents, and our best friends. I hold our entwined hands in the air and they cheer for us. It's been a long road to get here, but we made it. We're husband and wife, and I feel as though I can finally breathe deep and even.

I always thought that the day I was drafted to the professional league would be the happiest day of my life. I was wrong. Nothing will ever top the day I married my best friend.

The day that Reese Latham became Reese Reeves.

"Let's eat!" Nixon calls out, making everyone laugh.

Dinner is served in a private dining room with floor-to-ceiling windows that give us a perfect view of the ocean. Not that I've noticed. I can't take my eyes off my wife. She's glowing, and the smile on her face is permanent as she talks with our family. Our plates have long been cleared as we sit around and talk. I'm all for catching up with our loved ones, but right now, I need to love just one. My wife. I don't think I will ever get tired of saying that or hearing it.

"How much longer?" I whisper in her ear.

"Coop, they came all this way to celebrate with us."

I nod. "I know, and I love them for it, but right now, I need you. I need my wife," I say, kissing her bare shoulder. Goose bumps break out across her skin, and I give myself an internal fist bump.

"We have a lifetime, Coop."

She's right, but there is something primal in me that needs her now. The thought of making love to her as my wife has me shifting in my seat. I discreetly reach under the table and adjust my cock before placing my arm on the back of her chair. My girl wants to sit and chat with family, I can do that.

For her.

I hope she doesn't plan on getting much sleep tonight, though.

Chapter 26

REESE

My husband can't seem to keep his hands off me. Not that I'm complaining. Our families keep giving us knowing looks, but none of them are excusing themselves. I feel guilty leaving them when they came all this way, though.

We've been sitting in this room for hours talking and catching up. Our parents have told story after story of when we were kids and how they knew this day would come. They all claim they knew this is how our story would unfold. Tessa and Nixon jump on the bandwagon immediately, telling their own stories.

"I knew the minute he told a girl our freshman year to hit the road that it was Reese. She was jealous, but our boy here didn't care. No one came before Reese." Nixon retells his version of the story.

Cooper shrugs next to me. "No one ever will."

"Your daughter," Garrett speaks up. He leans in and kisses Eve on the cheek. "The only thing that can rival it is your daughter."

"Or your son," my mom adds.

My husband glances over at me. "Maybe we should test that theory?" His voice is loud so all of them can hear him.

"Coop." I breathe his name.

He gives me a mischievous smile as he leans in and kisses me softly. "I'm ready when you are, Mrs. Reeves."

I don't know if we're there yet, but the thought of it alone has me turned on. Then again, maybe that's just him and his wandering hands. His hot breath against my skin and his sweet kisses. It's everything that is the man sitting next to me.

My husband.

Speaking of my husband, he stands from his chair. When he offers me his hand and a sexy smile, I take it, letting him help me to my feet. "Thank you for coming. We love you all. But… yeah, it's time for us to go." He gives me a heated look, but I don't miss the light shade of pink on his cheeks.

Hugs and well wishes are granted, and a whispered, "Go get 'em girl," from Tessa, and we're on the elevator riding up to our room.

Cooper is standing behind me, with his front to my back, arms wrapped tightly around my waist. We're both quiet as the enormity of what's about to happen takes over our thoughts. At least they take over mine.

The doors slide open, and with his hand in mine, he guides us down the hall to our suite. Calmly and casually, he reaches into his pocket for the keycard and unlocks our room. He bends down and lifts me in his arms, pushing through the door. Carrying me over the threshold. "We're going to have to do this again when we get home," he says huskily as we step into the room. He places me gently on my feet as I take in the room.

I hear an audible click and then his husky voice whispering my name. "Mrs. Reeves."

I turn to look up at him. "Mr. Reeves."

"Come here." I do as he says and walk toward him. "You are so beautiful and this dress…" He makes a humming sound from deep in his throat. "I don't want to ruin it, baby, but I need it off you. Now," he adds.

I can't help but think back to the last time I was with him in a wedding dress. He had no issue ripping that one. He must see the confusion in my eyes.

"You wore this dress for me. It's the dress you chose to wear the day you became a Reeves. I'll cherish it always." He presses a kiss to my bare shoulder. "Help me, Reese. I need you naked, baby."

I giggle and reach behind me, showing him the clasp behind my neck. His fingers replace mine as he manages to unhook it and peel the bodice down to my waist. "Son of a bitch? No bra? All fucking day you've been sitting next to me in this sexy scrap of material and no bra?"

"The back of my dress is open. What else was I supposed to do?" I chuckle.

"I don't know. I just figured there was something, but… nothing." He bends his head and captures a nipple in his mouth. He nips it with his teeth before sucking hard.

"Oh, God," I moan.

"Naked, Mrs. Reeves," he says, his voice gravelly.

Hands on his shoulders, I push him away from me. Carefully, I step out of my dress and toss it over a chair to be dealt with later. Next, I move to the barefoot sandals.

"These are sexy as hell," he says, dropping to his knees and assisting me with their removal.

"Naked, Mr. Reeves," I say, pointing to his shirt and pants.

"Happy wife, happy life." He winks and strips out of his clothes.

I stand to take him in my hand, but he steps back. "You can't touch me. Not right now," he says. "Panties. Be gentle with them."

"Why?" I ask, sliding the sheer material over my thighs and down my legs.

"I'm keeping them."

"Coop, that's crazy."

"Not to me. You said I do in those panties. In my eyes, they are just as sacred as that dress over there." He points to the chair.

I toss my panties to the chair and hold my hands out at my sides. "I'm naked, Mr. Reeves. Now, what are you going to do with me?"

"On the bed," he demands. I comply and climb on the bed. "I had this plan. It was a great plan. In my head, we came back to the room. I slowly undressed you. Kissed every inch of your skin, and made love to you for hours." He strokes his hard length. I watch closely as he closes his eyes and takes a few deep breaths. All the while, his hand makes smooth, even strokes. "I can't do it, Reese. I can't. I want to go slow, but every fiber of my being is telling me to take what's mine."

"Coop." His name is merely a whisper as my body heats from his words. "Cooper," I try again. This time, his eyes snap open and land on mine. "I'm yours. Take me."

"It's our wedding night."

"We have every night for the rest of our lives. Besides, I know you. No way are you one and done."

"Fuck no."

"Take me."

He nods, climbing on the bed and settling between my thighs. "All day, Reese. All day I've thought about this moment. Why does it feel different, baby? It's us. But it feels like so much more."

"It is more. I'm now a Reeves."

"Damn right you are." His eyes are hooded as he aligns himself at my entrance.

"I love you, Mr. Reeves."

"I love you too, Mrs. Reeves," he replies as he pushes inside me. "Oh, fuck."

I wrap my arms and legs around him. I hold on as tight as I can. I don't need sweet and slow. I just need him. I just need my husband. "Coop, I need you."

"I'm right here. I wish I could tell you what this feels like. I wish I had the words to show you how intoxicated I am by you. Knowing that you're my wife." He shakes his head.

"Show me."

"Reese, you don't know what you're asking."

"Show me how it feels."

"I feel unhinged. The adrenaline coursing through my veins."

"You're always being easy with me, taking it slow. I want that passion, Cooper. I want to feel it."

"I need to treasure you."

"You can treasure me after you fuck me."

He hisses at my words. "Like this?" He pulls out and slams back in.

"Just like that," I say, barely keeping my eyes from rolling into the back of my head as he thrusts again.

"Mine," he growls as he unleashes. All I can do is hold on tight as he thrusts harder and faster.

Over and over again, he pounds into me, and it's the best sex we've ever had. I don't know if it's because I know he's mine, and I'm his, or if he's been holding back on me all this time, but it's not long before I feel the pressure start to build.

"You're squeezing my cock." He bears down on his bottom lip as he swivels his hips.

That one little move has my body igniting into flames as waves and waves of pleasure crash throughout my entire body. I feel like there is fire in my veins as I fall off the cliff into oblivion.

"Reese!" he shouts my name as his body stills, and he empties inside me.

His chest is heaving as he lowers his forehead to mine. "Holy shit," he pants.

"You've been holding out on me."

"I didn't know," he says, sucking in breath. "Did I hurt you?" He pulls back to look me in the eye.

"No." I cradle his face in my hands. "That was… incredible. I've never, you know," I say, feeling shy all of a sudden.

"You've never what?"

"It was intense. It's never been like that. Never felt like that."

"For me too," he says, kissing me sweetly. He rolls over to lie next to me, tugging me into his arms. "I need a minute to catch my breath, but then I'm going to make love to my wife."

"We could do that, or you know, repeat the previous performance," I suggest.

He laughs, his entire body shaking. "I love you so much."

"I love you too."

We lie here in each other's arms, just enjoying being together before he rolls over and makes good on his promise. He makes love to me. We shower and fall into bed, an exhausted, happy tangle of limbs.

This is our life.

This is bliss.

COOPER

The Defenders didn't make it to the Bowl this year, but that's okay. We had a hell of a season with only two losses until we got into the playoffs. It was a damn good season, one I'm proud as hell to be a part of.

Something else I'm proud to be a part of is the duo that is made up of me and my beautiful wife. It's the second week of February, and we're in Fiji on our honeymoon. This was supposed to be the week we were getting married, but we just couldn't wait that long. So here we are, a little over three months into our wedded bliss and relaxing on the beach.

"We didn't get to do this last time we were here," Reese says.

Her eyes are closed as she lounges in a bikini that should be illegal in all countries.

"We had more important things to do," I remind her. Not just getting married but staying in bed all day the day after. I refused to let her leave. I didn't care that our friends and family were here. I just needed some time with my wife. Time that she graciously agreed to. I took shit about it from Nixon, and I could see the glint in my father's eyes as we said goodbye at the airport. Hers gave me a look. Not really a warning, but something similar. It said "take care of her." I couldn't imagine being in his shoes and knowing that my daughter was…. Yeah, don't want to go there.

"What are you thinking so hard about over there?"

"About how much I love you." Not a complete lie, as that's all I think about. How I came close to losing the best fucking thing that ever happened to me. She's never not on my mind. Never.

"Look at you being all sweet."

"When am I not?" She lowers her glasses to her nose and gives me a heated look. "Baby, even when I'm fucking you, I'm sweet," I counter, making her laugh. I love the sound of her laugh. No one can make her laugh like I do.

"Don't give me that look, Cooper Reeves. I need a break, and you promised me some time in the sun."

"Fine," I concede. Even I'm a little dehydrated and drained from all the sex we've been having. I can't seem to help myself when it comes to her. I don't get to spend nearly enough time with her during the season. I'm trying to make up for that. And this is where she took my last name. This place alone does something to my libido.

"I talked to Tessa. They fly out tomorrow."

"It'll be good to see them."

"Definitely. They're going to start trying for a baby."

"Really?"

"Yep. She's really excited. Nixon too."

"Maybe we should try?" I toss the idea out there.

She turns to look at me, pushing her glasses on the top of her head. "I can't wait until we do, but I think we need a little more time. I have so much with the foundation, and it's just starting to get off the ground." My face falls, and she reaches over and places her hands on my arm. "That doesn't mean we can't keep practicing."

"There's never going to be a good time."

"I agree, but when we do decide to try, I'd like to try to make it happen so that when I deliver, you're home. I want you there."

"Yeah," I agree. My wife knows me well enough to understand that if she were to go into labor during a game, I'd say fuck the game. There is nothing in this life that is more important than her.

We're still young. We have plenty of time, but the thought of her carrying our baby, that turns me on like nothing else can.

"Coop." Her voice is raspy as her eyes lock in on my hardening cock. "Stop thinking about it." She laughs. The husky sound washes over me.

"I can't help myself, Mrs. Reeves." I smile at her. We've been married for a few months and I still can't stop calling her that. I don't think I'll ever tire of it.

"You drive a hard bargain with just that look." She points at me. "But that…" Her eyes drop to my cock. "That ups the ante."

"I'm good with practice," I tell her, wagging my eyebrows.

I want a family with her, but I know she has so much she wants to do with the foundation. As long as she knows that I'm ready when she is. I won't pressure her, but if I've learned anything over the years, it's to be transparent with her about what I want. Her. Our kids. Our life together. What more could a man ask for?

REESE

He has no idea how hard it is for me to tell him we're not ready just yet. I want nothing more than to start our family. At the same time, this foundation is my baby. He created this for me, and together, with his support, we're building something incredible that is going to help thousands of children in need.

"So, this summer?" he asks.

"What about this summer?"

"We start trying?"

"How many are we talking?" I ask him.

"At least two. I mean, if you're willing, we can try for a football team." He gives me a huge grin and a wink to go with it.

"Um, no." I chuckle.

"Two maybe four."

"Two to four, huh?"

"Can you get on board with that, Mrs. Reeves?"

"Yes."

He nods. "No pressure, baby. I just want you to know where my head is at. I can't wait to make babies with you."

"I want that too." In life there are no guarantees, and it's too short to keep putting off the things you can do today until tomorrow. I want to live every moment with him. That includes building our family. "This summer," I agree.

"Yeah?" I don't know that I've ever seen his smile so wide.

"Yes. That gives me time to hire more help with the foundation, and then we'll start trying."

He moves from his lounger to mine, pulling me on top of him. "Tell me about the foundation. Where are we?" Just like that, he's putting on his supportive husband hat. He's always willing to listen and offer suggestions, but he leaves the major decisions to me. What he doesn't realize is that I value his opinion. It's not just me, but us who's building this foundation. Together we're making a difference.

"I have so many plans. We're going to give all the kids a bag of their own for their belongings. I want to do social trips, individual shopping trips to get them the essentials. Make hygiene, such as haircuts, a priority to make them feel better about themselves." I stop and smile at him. "Sorry, I get carried away."

"I love your heart, Reese Reeves."

"You should. You keep it beating." The words are barely out of my mouth when his lips fuse to mine. He nips at my bottom lip, and I open for him. His hands roam my body, and I melt into his touch. He flips us over so my back is on the lounger as he hovers over me. His large muscled leg slides between mine, and I moan at the contact.

"We should take this back to the room."

"Not yet," I say breathlessly as I rock my hips against his thigh.

"Fuck," he moans. "In the room, now," he says, pulling away. His chest is rising and falling at a rapid pace as he stares down at me with nothing but desire in his eyes. "Come with me, Mrs. Reeves." He gathers our stuff in one arm and holds the other hand out for me.

Placing my hand in his, he guides us back to the room, and that's where we stay the remainder of the day.

Wrapped up in the sheets.

Our hearts entangled.

Bliss.

Thank you for taking the time to read

Bliss

and completing the Entangled Heart Duet.

Never miss a new release:
http://bit.ly/2UW5Xzm

More about Kaylee's books:
http://bit.ly/2CV3hLx

Contact
KAYLEE RYAN

Facebook:
http://bit.ly/2C5DgdF

Instagram:
http://bit.ly/2reBkrV

Reader Group:
http://bit.ly/2o0yWDx

Goodreads:
http://bit.ly/2HodJvx

BookBub:
http://bit.ly/2KulVvH

Website:
www.kayleeryan.com

Other works by KAYLEE RYAN

With You Series:
Anywhere With You | More With You | Everything With You

Soul Serenade Series:
Emphatic | Assured | Definite | Insistent

Southern Heart Series:
Southern Pleasure | Southern Desire | Southern Attraction | Southern Devotion

Unexpected Arrivals Series:
Unexpected Reality | Unexpected Fight
Unexpected Fall | Unexpected Bond | Unexpected Odds

Standalone Titles:
Tempting Tatum | Unwrapping Tatum | Levitate
Just Say When | I Just Want You
Reminding Avery | Hey, Whiskey | When Sparks Collide
Pull You Through | Beyond the Bases
Remedy | The Difference
Trust the Push

Co-written with Lacey Black:
It's Not Over | Just Getting Started | Can't Fight It

Cocky Hero Club:
Lucky Bastard

Acknowledgements

To my readers:
We did it! We survived my very first duet. I wasn't sure I would be able to write a cliff hanger. You know me, I like things to be tied up nice and neat with a bow at the end. My only saving grace was that I wrote both books at the same time. Thank you for hanging in there with me.

To my family:
Thank you for being by my side through all of this. I could not do this without your support. I love you.

Braadyn Pendrod:
I gave you a concept, and titles that's all you had to go off of and you nailed it! Thank you so much for the images for both Agony and Bliss. You captured Reese and Cooper perfectly.

Tami Integrity Formatting:
Thank you for making the paperbacks beautiful. You're amazing and I cannot thank you enough for all that you do.

Sommer Stein:
Time and time again, you wow me with your talent. Thank you for another amazing cover.

Lacey Black:
You are my sounding board, and I value that so very much. Thank you for always being there, talking me off the ledge and helping me jump from it when necessary.

My beta team:
Jamie, Stacy, Lauren, Erica, and Franci I would be lost without you. You read my words as much as I do, and I can't tell you what your input and all the time you give means to me. Countless messages and bouncing idea, you ladies keep me sane when the characters are being anything but. Thank you from the bottom of my heart for taking this wild ride with me.

Give Me Books:
With every release, your team works diligently to get my book in the hands of bloggers. I cannot tell you how thankful I am for your services.

Tempting Illustrations:
Thank you for everything. I would be lost without you.

Julie Deaton:
Thank you for giving this book a set of fresh final eyes.

Becky Johnson:
I could not do this without you. Thank you for pushing me, and making me work for it.

Marisa Corvisiero:
Thank you for all that you do. I know I'm not the easiest client. I'm blessed to have you on this journey with me.

Kimberly Ann:
Thank you for organizing and tracking the ARC team. I couldn't do it without you.

Bloggers:
Thank you, doesn't seem like enough. You don't get paid to do what you do. It's from the kindness of your heart and your love of reading that fuels you. Without you, without your pages, your voice, your reviews, spreading the word it would be so much harder if not impossible to get my words in reader's hands. I can't tell you how much your never-ending support means to me. Thank you for being you, thank you for all that you do.

To my Kick Ass Crew:

The name of the group speaks for itself. You ladies truly do KICK ASS! I'm honored to have you on this journey with me. Thank you for reading, sharing, commenting, suggesting, the teasers, the messages all of it. Thank you from the bottom of my heart for all that you do. Your support is everything!

With Love,

Kaylee Ryan

Made in the USA
Columbia, SC
17 January 2021